D0661148

A
Harlequin
Romance

OTHER

Harlequin Romances

by JANE ARBOR

919—DEAR INTRUDER
950—KINGFISHER TIDE
1000—A GIRL NAMED SMITH
1048—HIGH MASTER OF CLERE
1108—SUMMER EVERY DAY
1157—YESTERDAY'S MAGIC
1182—GOLDEN APPLE ISLAND
1277—STRANGER'S TRESPASS
1336—THE CYPRESS GARDEN
1406—WALK INTO THE WIND
1443—THE FEATHERED SHAFT
1480—THE LINDEN LEAF
1544—THE OTHER MISS DONNE
1582—WILDFIRE QUEST
1665—THE FLOWER ON THE ROCK
1740—ROMAN SUMMER
1789—THE VELVET SPUR
1832—MEET THE SUN HALFWAY

Many of these titles are available at your local bookseller,
or through the Harlequin Reader Service.

For a free catalogue listing all available Harlequin Romances,
send your name and address to:

HARLEQUIN READER SERVICE,
M.P.O. Box 707, Niagara Falls, N.Y. 14302
Canadian address: Stratford, Ontario, Canada.

or use order coupon at back of book.

THE WIDE FIELDS OF HOME

by

JANE ARBOR

HARLEQUIN BOOKS   TORONTO
WINNIPEG

Original hard cover edition published in 1975
by Mills and Boon Limited.

© Jane Arbor 1975

SBN 373-01896-7

Harlequin edition published July 1975

Printed in Canada

1896

The author gratefully acknowledges the help of
technical advice from Mr. J. Lappin and Mr. H.
Jensen of Geest Industries Ltd. and from Mr. F.
Doerflinger of The Bulb Information Desk and
author of *The Bulb Book*.

CHAPTER ONE

'You are going to Amsterdam on holiday?"

The question came from the middle-aged lady occupying the middle seat of one of the banks of three on that side of the aircraft cabin. Beyond her, next to the aisle, was a man who, immediately on take-off, had pulled down his table and used it for a bulging briefcase, topped by *Punch* and *The Times*. He was folding the latter for convenience of reading as Jonnet, in the window seat, turned her head. Their eyes met briefly. She registered that he was a young giant, very fair, with wide blue eyes; then his stranger's glance dismissed her and her own went to her questioner.

"On holiday?" she echoed. "Oh no. Just on a – duty visit. And not to Amsterdam itself. To stay with an aunt who lives in the country about ten miles south-west of the city." Feeling this was all the information politeness required of her, she resumed her dispirited contemplation of the daunting scene beyond the rain-lashed windows.

People's homes turning to mere dolls' houses as the aircraft climbed; flooded acreages becoming ponds; grey cloud piled upon grey cloud, and then – nothing but the vicious rain and no horizon at all.

Holiday! In the first days of January, and bound for a wind and water-girt country probably even more dreary than the wintry England she was leaving behind? Holiday indeed! She would dearly have liked to retort to the kindly question, "You must be joking!" for anything less promising than her present errand to her present mood she could not imagine.

Her companion settled herself after undoing her seatbelt, took some knitting from a holdall. "Well, I'm not really on holiday myself," she announced. "And I'm only staying one night in Amsterdam, then going on to Brussels to my married daughter while she has a baby. But – to your aunt? Then I expect you've been to Holland before?"

"No. Yes –" Jonnet corrected herself. "I was taken when I was very small, but I don't remember that."

"And is your aunt Dutch or English?"

"Dutch. My father's elder sister."

Working that out and appraising Jonnet's dark grey eyes and the pageboy cut of her corn-coloured hair, "Then you are Dutch yourself? Of course, your colouring – Though, you know, I wouldn't have guessed."

"You would have been wrong if you had," Jonnet retorted too shortly. "I'm English. I was born in England and I've always lived there. It's just that my brother is living with my aunt while he is teaching English in a school in Amsterdam, so I'm visiting him too."

"Oh." A moment or two's recovery from the rebuff in Jonnet's tone, then her companion battled on. "That will be nice for you. You'll enjoy that –"

"In *January*?"

"Why not? Well, skating, you know, and all that – I believe they enjoy their winter, the Dutch. Besides, if you're staying for a while, it won't always be January –"

"I'm not staying for long."

"– and Holland is such a very *picturesque* country, I always say," concluded the other, valiantly achieving her point in face of the odds against her.

"*Do* you? I'd call it merely quaint myself."

"Yes, well – quaint too, of course –"

"Trading on its image." At the sudden stir and crackle of *The Times* from the aisle-seat, Jonnet was made aware that she had a second listener to her reckless abandonment

8

of good manners, and didn't care. "Clogs. And canals. And Dutch bonnets. And windmills. With a touch of smuggled diamonds for spice. Whereas the reality – the men mostly a lot of podgy burghers, and the women a set of worthy housewives, making a thing of getting their spring-cleaning done before Easter!"

As soon as the vituperative catalogue ceased, partly for want of Jonnet's breath, she knew she deplored the silly prejudice of the words, and was ashamed. But they had been the expression of all her reluctance for today's errand, and they were out. She couldn't take them back, and at least she had the consolation that in less than a couple of hours' time she wouldn't have either to enlarge upon them or eat them before these two strangers whom she was never likely to meet again after their journey's end at Schiphol Airport.

Meanwhile, neither of her fellow passengers seemed disposed to force her to make a meal of such generalised nonsense. The knitting-needles clicked quietly on, and from the corner of her eye Jonnet saw Aisle-Seat take a fountain-pen from an inner pocket and begin on *The Times* Crossword. After a minute or two Knitting-Needles said mildly, "Well, you do have some strong views of a country you don't know, I must say." Aisle-Seat said nothing at all, and for the rest of the flight Jonnet was left to her chosen, brooding silence.

Too late she had regretting yielding to the nag of conscience which had made her agree to join her brother Dirk for a stay at Tante Grethe's homestead. After her long months of nursing their widower father until his death, and the tedious legal processes of sharing the proceeds of his small estate between Dirk and herself, she felt she had deserved better of her fate than a winter trip to Holland instead of a fortnight in the Caribbean which friends had

9

offered her after she had promised Dirk.

She had taken some persuading that it was her belated duty to make Tante Grethe's acquaintance. But with unexpected spirit Dirk, who usually fell in with her plans for them both, not she with his, had adroitly turned her own earlier argument against her.

"When I got the job in Amsterdam, it was you who made me get in touch with Tante Grethe and try to bury whatever hatchet there was between her and Father, by suggesting I might live with her in term-time, if she'd have me," he had reminded her.

"Yes, well, it was a good idea, wasn't it?" Jonnet had countered. "She doesn't charge you as much as you would have to pay in city digs, and I thought it was high time someone from this side of the family got to know her."

"And she welcomed me, which makes one more reason why I think you should take the friendly mitt she's offered *you* by inviting you to go over, now you are free," Dirk had retorted.

"But Holland in mid-winter! And I wanted to go to the *sun*. Besides, I'm not as free as all that. I've got to try to get my old job back or find another," Jonnet objectted.

But with a "Phooey! You can afford to live on your fat, or I'll finance you for a fortnight or so," Dirk had demolished that argument with brotherly crudity, and she had given in, knowing in her heart that he was right. Besides, that it had been her original idea to make contact with their aunt had made his reasoning the easier to take. For she had always prided herself on arriving at her own decisions and standing by them, wise or not. The-Boy-Stood-On-The-Burning-Deck mentality, Dirk called it, teasing her. But, though at twenty-four he was three years her senior, he hadn't often crossed her and only rarely had she had to allow that a bit of giving-in and flexibility had their virtues too . . .

Dirk's initiation into Dutch life had been at the beginning of the previous autumn school term, so that by now Jonnet knew much of Grethe Handel's circumstances. That, at sixty years old, she still ran the Handel family bulb-farm, from her homestead on the estate. Her elder brother, Hans, had died in his early twenties, and now that Pieter Handel, Jonnet's and Dirk's father, was dead, all that remained of the Handel family were Grethe and her younger sister, Letti, twice widowed, with a stepdaughter named Saskia. By her second husband Letti was wealthy, and she and Saskia lived in Amsterdam. Until Dirk had joined her, Grethe had managed the farm alone, served both in the house and about the estate by a character of indefinable old age, named, simply, Munt.

"If he has a Christian name, I've never heard it," Dirk had reported. "If Tante Grethe had an indoor staff, he would be its major-domo, I suppose. As it is, he's a kind of John Brown to her Queen Victoria, and they fit like a pair of scissors-blades, no less."

Dirk had met Tante Letti and Saskia quite often. They orbited mostly in Amsterdam circles. Letti he described as "fiftyish and limp" and Saskia as "a dishy kitten" of nineteen. She hadn't a job, didn't need one; Letti could afford to keep her as her "darling girl", though she wasn't in fact. Letti had only inherited her with her second husband, Klaus Moet.

In looks Grethe was as round as a dumpling and, according to Dirk, in character about as cosy as a ball of steel. Jonnet gathered she had not minced her criticism of their father for leaving Holland to go to England as a motor-engineer, and Dirk had had to counter in his defence that surely, if he had known he didn't want to be a bulb-farmer, he had had the right to choose his own career. But her bitterness once voiced, as Dirk had urged on Jonnet, she had welcomed him in her fashion, and he suspected she was glad they had made a move which her pride wouldn't allow her to make herself.

Dirk had bought a small car for commuting daily into the city, and Jonnet, picturing her stay, hoped she might often be able to go with him. For her brash criticism of "quaint" didn't include Amsterdam. From her reading and from what she had seen on screen and in pictures she allowed that Amsterdam was beautiful. She glanced covertly at her two companions, thought a little shamefacedly, "Perhaps I ought to say so; admit I must have sounded pretty sour without cause."

But from their absorption in, respectively, their knitting and their crossword puzzle, it seemed they didn't want to know. And then, shortly afterwards, it was already too late. A change in the beat of the aircraft's engines preluded its descent and it was time for the fastening of seat-belts and readiness for the disembarkation which would send them all on their separate ways.

The wind tearing across the tarmac was cruel. Topcoat collar high, head down to the blast, Jonnet caught no further glimpse of her seat-mates after the air hostess had led the way to the Customs Hall. And when she had collected her luggage Dirk was there, greeting her, asking about the flight and taking her out to the car park. As he stowed her things in the boot of his car she shivered visibly.

"I suppose it blows pretty often like this?" she asked.

Dirk opened the door for her. "Get in. Yes. What do you expect? We're below sea-level here, and it comes straight off the Arctic."

"How do you stand it?"

"I don't know. Perhaps having some Dutch blood helps. Anyway, one gets used to it. I have."

Jonnet shivered again. "Well, rather you than me for any length of time," she said.

"Yes, well –" Dirk began, and stopped.

"What were you going to say?"

"Nothing. Except to ask how you think they would have got power for their windmills, if there hadn't always been the wind to drive them?"

"Maybe. But what are electricity and gas and oil for? The windmills are only part of the legend now, aren't they?"

"Not all of them. Some of them are still worked in the country. There's one not far from Tante Grethe's –"

Jonnet switched direction. "And if you're defending the wind, does that mean that you like it here?"

Dirk said mildly, "You needn't make an accusation of it. If I hadn't thought I should like it, I needn't have come, need I?"

"But *do* you?" Jonnet pressed.

He nodded. "Yes. It grows on you, wind and all. Since I've been here I can't think why we never made the parents bring us, or came ourselves –"

"I never wanted to, particularly," Jonnet put in.

Dirk went on, "It was Father's prejudice, I suppose. He must have passed some of it to you. But let's face it, to the extent to which we're half-Dutch, it's at least half as much our home country as England is. And thank goodness they let us be bi-lingual. You'll find it helps, and I couldn't have held down my job if I weren't. As for Amsterdam – just wait to see it. You'll fall flat on your face for it, as I did."

Jonnet allowed, "I hope so. It'll have to make up for a lot. But I suppose I shall *have* to wait until you're free to

13

show it to me? We don't touch it on our way to Tante Grethe's today, do we?"

"Not officially. The farm is about the same distance out as Schiphol, but more westerly, south of Haarlem." Dick waved a vague hand. "Anyway, we're headed for the city now."

"Oh, why? Or should I say 'Good' – putting off the Tante Grethe confrontation?" Jonnet enquired.

Dirk laughed. "She's not as difficult as all that. It's just a case of needing to break the ice –"

"In this temperature, how apt!" murmured Jonnet, and Dirk laughed again.

"You *have* made up your mind to crab everything in sight, haven't you?" he countered. He went on, "You deserve to have to write an essay in Dutch on the theme I gave one of my classes this morning. Want to hear? *Een by zonder angel maakt geen honing.* Now what does that mean?"

Jonnet translated smoothly, "A bee without a sting makes no honey,' I think."

"Exactly. In other words, 'You gotta take the rough with the smooth, girl, *and* like it – or else!' However, you asked, Why Amsterdam? and I'm telling you, Wait till we get there."

For answer Jonnet tucked her face deeper into her coat collar and watched in silence as the flat open terrain gave place to the neat suburban streets south of the city, to one or two wintry-looking public parks and so to wider avenues of finer houses and buildings and then to the first of the canals which ringed the city centre about.

Jonnet sat up then. This was indeed beginning to be the Amsterdam of the colour supplements and Wish You Were Here picture-postcards from tourist friends. It was much warmer here than on that bleak prairie they had crossed;

it was still early afternoon, but the street and shop lights were on, and wherever there was water, there were reflections which danced and shimmered and mischievously broke up solid shapes. And there was water – everywhere.

A restaurant window displaying luscious chocolates and cream cakes caught her eye. "I could do with some tea," she murmured. "If you could find somewhere to park, couldn't we stop?"

But Dirk said, "All in good time. We're nearly there. And now –" pausing to negotiate a difficult turn designed to slide the car into the narrow space between two others facing sheer on to the canal – "now we are. We're here." He braked and switched off, then twisted in his seat to gesture behind him. "That's here," he said in obscure explanation.

Following his jerked thumb, Jonnet looked behind and up – a long way up – at the tall mansion behind a shading of plane trees which was as typical of elegant Dutch architecture of an earlier century as any she had ever seen.

It was at least four storeys high, with windows also in the gabled façade of the roof. It was of warm red stone with white facings. The highest, central gable was flanked by pairs of two others, stepping down in tiers. The roof-lines of its neighbours and of the buildings beyond them were all of different heights, set in cut-out against a sky which had suddenly turned to a pale, cold blue. But it was a palace it had to be! What had it to do with Dirk or he with it? Now someone had to be joking.

"What do you mean?" she demanded of him. "That house – I suppose it is a house? What is it?"

"You'll see," he promised. "Come along. We're going in."

They both got out of the car and she waited while he used a key on a narrow ground-floor door flanking a wider main door. Inside, an open door to a sitting-room and another to a kitchen suggested a self-contained flat, and when Jonnet said blankly, "It's a flat," Dirk nodded.

"Clever girl. What's more, it's mine," he said, and then, at her frown of bewilderment, hastily pushed her inside the living-room which had a tiny dining alcove, and said, "But you wanted tea. I'll get it and explain while we have it. Want to wash or anything? There's a bathroom too."

But Jonnet wasn't having that – abandoned until he chose to explain himself! She followed him into the kitchen and stood over him while he laid up a tray and put on a kettle.

"Look," she said, "what is this? You're living with Tante Grethe. What do you want with a flat, and how did you get it?"

"Yes, well, I was living with Tante Grethe," he admitted. "I'm not any more."

"Why not?"

"Well, I'd been with her for three months, all last term, and it wasn't very convenient for school – evening activities and all that. And as you were coming over, and I got the chance of this place –" He broke off to make the tea and carried the tray into the living-room, leaving Jonnet to follow. She took her tea from him and stirred it, but didn't drink.

"You mean you've rented it? As a permanency?" she asked.

"I've signed a year's lease. At a very low rent – almost peppercorn."

"So that you won't be out at the farm while I'm there? Why didn't you tell me?"

"No. I ought to have told you, but I wanted to surprise you. And I shouldn't have left Tante Grethe's, if you hadn't been coming to take my place."

"For a fortnight? If you had any scruples about leaving

16

Tante Grethe, how did that help?"

Dirk stirred uncomfortably. "Look," he said. "You don't know it all, so let me explain. I haven't quarrelled with the aunt, and she didn't throw me out. But commuting from out there was tedious; conscience about my being out late sometimes meant I couldn't join in anything social in the city. And when this chap, Axel Keyser – you know I've mentioned him?"

"Yes. He owns the land next to the Boerdery Handel, you said."

"*And* this house. His family has owned it since 'way back. Like ours, his parents are dead. He isn't married, but he lives here, in all the rest of the house."

Jonnet thought of the storeys above them. "He must rattle," she commented.

"He's got money. He entertains a lot."

"And what does he do?"

"He runs his estate. Anyway, as I was saying, when I got to know him, he saw I had a problem, and when he heard you were coming over, he offered me this place, saying it would oblige him to have someone in it, and that as Tante Grethe would have you staying with her instead of me, I needn't have a conscience."

"Which shows, I'd say, that the two of you must be out of your infant minds. This Keyser person offers you a year's lease; you take it; *I* plan to stay a matter of a couple of weeks at the farm. Where does it all fit in?" Jonnet asked.

Dirk hesitated. "Well, like this – if you see it as we do. When I told Axel how you were placed – about the long time you were nursing Father, and after that, all the business of selling up, of which you did the most; and that you weren't yet committed to another job and that you deserved a long break, he said –"

17

Jonnet sat forward, forcing a smile. "Do tell me. I can hardly wait!" she said.

Dirk's glance was anxious. "You're mad at us, and you've no reason to be. We were thinking of you as much as of me."

"I'm *sure*. But go on. What did this big-hearted meddler say?"

"I've told you. That I oughtn't to let you make difficulties about staying on for, say, a few months. That he would see Tante Grethe would expect you to, and that, for your own sake, you should be glad of the chance to see what kind of a spring and summer show Holland can lay on. Besides," Dirk appealed, "*I* love the country, and I'd like to share more of it with you than I could in a mere couple of weeks."

"Then you could have asked me yourself: warned me you were going to, instead of springing it on me at the say-so of this —!" Struck suddenly by the full enormity of the high-handed disposal of her person and her time, Jonnet found herself at a loss for outraged words, and as she paused, panting with indignation, there was a sound as of the opening and closing of the main door of the house.

Dirk said quickly, "That will be Axel now. You must meet him," and as if glad of momentary escape, he went through a connecting door from the tiny hall and came back followed by the very last man Jonnet wanted or could have expected to see. Aisle-Seat in person!

Across the little room the blue eyes, brilliantly alive, met her own as they had done so briefly on the aircraft. But this time they lingered in instant recognition of her, and in the same moment as her thoughts raced, *Punch? The Times* Crossword? *That man was English!* His wryly amused voice clashed with Dirk's introduction, saying, in English with scarcely a touch of foreign inflection, "Well, well! Our

Captious Critic herself. So I did put two and two together, making five, after all!" and he held out his hand to her.

She touched it with polite fingers. "How do you do?" she said. Dirk looked from one to the other, then back to his friend.

"What do you mean – 'two and two'?" he puzzled. "You haven't met Jonnet before, have you – anywhere?"

The other two began speaking together. Jonnet's voice came frostily, "As a matter of fact –" but gave way before the man's "In a manner of speaking, yes. And no. We formed two of a threesome on our plane, another English lady between us."

"On your –?" Dirk snapped his fingers. "Of course! You've been over to England. I forgot. But 'two and two'? Do you mean that on the way over you guessed who Jonnet was?"

Axel Keyser shook his head. "I'm not clairvoyant. But, eavesdropping, I had an idea she was telling me, via our companion. Going to stay with an aunt ... A brother teaching in Amsterdam ... Virtually her first visit, one gathered, though –"

As he broke off and his glance went from Dirk to her, Jonnet stared back at him, challenging him, *daring* him to repeat to Dirk the inanities her frustration had uttered, allowing him to overhear. In an instant of dumb show between them she watched his brows lift in question, then she lowered her glance and looked away. Without the use of words he had asked, "You don't want me to tell?" and, mortified at having to plead with him, she had answered, "Please don't."

He didn't. But when, to Dirk's question of, "But if you thought you had a clue, why didn't you speak to her, make yourself known?" he glanced her way again and said, "I didn't dare," she thought she had misread his promise and

19

he was going to betray her to Dirk after all.

But he only went on, "For instance, if this girl hadn't been Jonnet, where should I have been then, my friend?" and when Dirk retorted, "If I know you, in *full* command of the situation!" they both laughed, leaving Jonnet out.

Axel looked down at the table. "Tea?" he said. "Thank you for asking me. Yes, please. And *koekjes* too." He chose a biscuit and bit into it, and Dirk took up the pot.

"We've been having a row, and we haven't been drinking ours. I'll make some fresh," he said, and went back to the kitchen to get it.

Axel Keyser sat down, draping an arm over the back of his chair and disposing his long legs comfortably. "A row?" he enquired with mild interest. "That's a pity. What was it about?"

Jonnet said, "I should think you might know. It was at least partly about your unwarranted interference in my affairs."

"As Dirk's friend. Someone had to put his case for him. Making a permanency of living out at the Boerdery Handel, he would be impossibly hamstrung in his social life."

"Though I doubt if he believed he had a 'case', until you pointed it out to him. And I suppose it was also your idea that I shouldn't hear of your plans until after I arrived?"

As if he expected her to agree with him, he said disarmingly, "Well, the *fait accompli* is popularly believed to have some strength, isn't it? And though it was Dirk's own way of playing for safety, when I heard you making public your views on my country's shortcomings, I confess I decided we had been right to corner you first and argue afterwards!"

Jonnet said coldly, "I see. Two against one, and all cut-and-dried beforehand."

20

"Three against one," he corrected. "Grethe Handel approves the arrangement."

"Primed by you, I gather. Dirk said —"

But she broke off as Dirk, returning with the tea, looked anxiously from her to Axel. "Have you explained things to her, why we did it?" he asked his friend.

Axel shrugged. "It's uphill work. Your sister is convinced of Conspiracy with a capital C."

"Yes, well, it was the only way." Dirk turned to Jonnet. "I suppose you'll admit that if I'd told you that Tante Grethe was expecting you to stay in my place, you wouldn't have come?"

"I'd have come for the fortnight I'd promised you." A sense of ill-usage made Jonnet's lip quiver as she added, "I think you might have — have trusted me about the rest."

Dirk said contritely, using his pet name for her, "Oh, Jon, I'm sorry. But we did do it for you too." He poured the tea and they drank in silence. Only Axel selected and ate biscuits with apparent enjoyment.

Presently Dirk looked at his watch and said, "I think we must be going, Jon, if I'm to get back in time for a staff meeting that's been called at school for tonight." Upon which Axel asked the time of the meeting and on hearing, said, "You'll be cutting it fine if you're to get back. I'm going out to my own place, and if your sister will permit it, I can deliver her to the farm and make your excuses to your aunt."

Still disposing of me as if I were a parcel! thought Jonnet, but she agreed with as much grace as she could muster, and they left the house together, parting from Dirk at the parked cars. As Axel drove south again across the city, he pointed out landmarks and the direction of others. "The Dam, the city's heart; the Muntplein; the Flower Market. To the left, the Rijksmuseum; passing the Vondelpark . . ."

21

As they left the city behind Jonnet made conversation, admiring his house and asking how he was placed there.

"I have a woman named Marthe who comes in morning and evening, and I regard is as my centre. But I have what you would call in England a 'pad' out on my place which marches with your aunt's, and I can camp out there on occasion when I need to."

Jonnet said politely, "You speak English like an Englishman. In fact, I thought you were one."

"I go over to England a lot, and we Dutch make English our second language from our schooldays on." He slanted a smile at her. "And I gathered – at least I hoped – you mightn't have been quite as offensive as you sounded, if you had supposed a Dutchman to be listening in."

Jonnet flushed scarlet. "Of course I shouldn't. I'm not *quite* a boor."

"No. Just an opinionated, prejudiced know-it-all."

Roused afresh, she retorted, "If you say so. Though if you were offended, I wonder you didn't tell Dirk what I had said. Why didn't you?"

He seemed to consider the question. Then he said, "Well, I'm not one myself, but I imagine the butterfly-collector allows his victim to flutter briefly on its pin before he uses the killing-bottle on it, don't you?"

"In other words, you enjoyed seeing me flutter?"

"I felt you deserved to. But don't worry. I shan't report on you to Dirk. Such education about the real Holland as I think you need, I'm prepared to give you myself."

The consummate nerve of the man! "Indeed? You – and who else?" Jonnet mocked.

He shook his head. "I shan't need help. When you go back to England, you'll take with you a less jaundiced view of our country, or I'll know the reason why."

"All in a fortnight? Won't it be rather a crash course?"

"Ah, but you are staying longer than a fortnight, *mejuf-rouw*."

"Really? Are you making a ruling on that too?"

"No. But your moral sense towards your aunt should, and if it needs any prodding, I'll do it." He stopped the car on a road which ran away into the winter dusk, as flat and empty as a stretched ribbon. He half-turned in his seat. "Look," he urged, "this has to be said, so why not by me? And so – Dirk, I know, is twenty-four. How old are you?"

"Just twenty-one."

"Exactly. Both of you adult, earning your own livings but guilty of owing a lot of time to Grethe Handel. Why haven't you got in touch with her until now?"

"We weren't encouraged to. Our father was estranged from her, and she never made a move towards *us*."

"With your father's refusal to come back to run the family business when his brother died, she felt she had a legitimate grievance against him. And as I see it, it has always been up to you two to heal any rift there was. Well, at least Dirk seems to have had a belated prick of conscience –"

"Yes, but Dirk –" Jonnet began.

As she stopped short, her companion waited. But she only shook her head. "Nothing," she evaded. "Go on." For sheer stubborn pride's sake she would not plead with him that it had been she, not Dirk, who had urged the move to peace. If he chose to assume she had been lacking in charity to Tante Grethe, then let him!

He was silent for a moment, then went on, "And so, as Dirk has done his part to date, it seems only justice to him and your aunt that you should do yours."

"At any inconvenience to me?"

He nodded gravely. "At *any*, I'd say," he confirmed adding as he started the car again, "Dirk, for one, is going to be very disappointed in you if you don't."

That was all. Of course his "for one" had only been a figure of speech; he must know, mustn't he? that only Dirk's disappointment would count with her, thought Jonnet. And yet if he had pinioned her by the wrists and physically forced her to agree, he could not have made his own will more evident. What was even more strange was that, for all her reluctance, he had left her with an inability to say an outright "No" to him.

Why couldn't she? To find herself so — so *pliant* was a new sensation, and she didn't like it. There was no reason in the world why she should yield to his perusasion; no reason at all why she should worry about his judgment of her if she didn't. All she knew was that, by some magnetic pull which she resented, he had swayed her the way he wanted, and that when he asked her — as he surely would — what her decision was, she would give in.

He didn't ask her. He drove in silence along the featureless road until he pointed across the bleak plain ahead to the outline of a house silhouetted against the sky. "That is your journey's end," he said.

"*That?*" She turned dismayed eyes on him. "But it's in the middle of nowhere! How am I ever going to get away from it or back to it?"

"If you're only staying a fortnight, no doubt Dirk will chauffeur you. Though — just supposing — you were thinking of staying longer, why not a bicycle? I suppose you can ride one?"

"Of course I can," she snapped.

"Then you'd have no problem. Very easy riding, as you can see. No hills. And you'd be in the popular swim — we all ride bicycles here. It's practically a national custom."

Jonnet said nothing to that, and his next remark as they neared the house was to say, "Beyond your aunt's holding — my land. You may just see the outline of my glasshouses and the estate buildings away to the right."

Jonnet sat forward and peered. "I don't –"

"No? It's probably too dark if you don't know where to look. Remind me to give you a conducted tour before you go back – if you can make time, that is. But here we are –"

Without benefit of hedge or other marked boundary the house stood square to the open field it faced. There was nothing else near it but the yard buildings which flanked it on one side. Its steeply pitched tiled roof sat on it like a red lid on a white box. The undrawn curtains to the windows were all dark crimson, and the only sign of welcome was a light in one of the groundfloor rooms.

Axel Keyser took Jonnet's luggage from the car to the stout unpretentious front door. "I'll see you safely delivered," he said. And then, before he used the heavy knocker, he added, "By the way, about that bicycle. Shall I ask Dirk to get you one or not?"

Jonnet had to moisten her dry lips. "You can tell him that – I think – I'd better have one," she said slowly. And sensed, without needing to look at him, that they both knew she had given him the answer he wanted to the question he hadn't asked.

CHAPTER TWO

THE door was answered by a white-haired woman who could only be Tante Grethe. In a brown fisherman's-knit pullover, tweed skirt and sturdy brogues, she was as squat as Dirk had described her. Her eyes were bright behind old-fashioned spectacles and her colour was rosy in a skin wrinkled like an ageing pippin.

Axel Keyser pulled an imaginary forelock to her. "Good evening, ma'am. Delivery – one English niece," he said in Dutch.

"So?" She stood aside to allow them in. "Where is Dirk? Why did he not bring her?" she asked in the same language.

Axel explained about Dirk's engagement, and the keen eyes took stock of Jonnet. "You are Jonnet? Do you speak and understand Dutch as well as Dirk does?" she asked.

"I think so."

"That is as well, for my English is not good, and my manager, Munt, has none." As Grethe spoke she showed them in to the lighted room where a table was laid for a cold meal of sliced meats, a cheese board and a bowl of fresh fruit. On a dresser of dark carved oak there were drinks and a coffee percolator on low thermostat bubbling quietly to itself. A fire of logs burned in the open grate; the sills of two windows were ranged with potted plants and if the bleak darkness outside had been curtained off – which it wasn't – the effect would have been wholly cosy.

Grethe gestured towards the bottles. "You will take a gin? Or eat with us?" she asked Axel.

He refused both the drink and the meal. "I'm driving,"

he said. "I won't stay." To Jonnet he added casually, "I come over most days, and I shall expect you to let me show you my place some time," and left, brushing aside her thanks for the drive from the city.

After showing him out Grethe brisked back and suggested Jonnet would like to go to her room before they had supper. Switching off the dining-room light as she put on those of the hall and landing, she said, "There is no economy in unnecessary lights, and we have to be careful" – which, as she was to find out later, Jonnet rightly read as a lesson she was expected to learn.

The bedroom in which she was left was also heavily furnished in old oak which would fetch a handsome price in any modern sale-room. The wardrobe and dresser were both spacious and there was a fitted washbasin. But there was no extra light over its mirror, nor was there one over the bed. Cringing at the thought of having to pad, barefoot, over to the switch at the door after a session of reading in bed, as an experiment Jonnet lit both the candles in their broad-based candlesticks standing on the dressing-table.

She was surprised and a little enchanted by the result. She had forgotten what the softness of candlelight could do for a girl's looks. . . . Efficient make-up might demand the white glare of electricity, but there was something *about* these unusual shadows and highlights touching cheekbones, deepening the colour of eyes and bringing out the sheen of hair. Watching her reflection in the mirror she wished she could think she always looked like that to people. For instance, to anyone meeting her for the first time . . . anyone who, in the cold fact of daylight, saw only a run-of-the-mill dark blonde with stone-grey eyes and – today possibly – a rather stubborn mouth. When she was ready to go downstairs again, she blew out the candles with regret.

The supper table was laid with only two places, Grethe

explaining that though the as yet unseen Munt lived in the house, he chose to eat alone and sometimes to cook for himself. Over the meal, which was good, Jonnet realised what Dirk had meant by likening their aunt to a ball of steel. She had not once uttered the word Welcome, though possibly implying it by her assumption that Jonnet had plenty of time before her, and by her questions as to the comfort of her journey and whether she liked her room. Other questions – about the sold-up home in England and about Jonnet's late job as a junior librarian – she put in abruptly between Jonnet's own polite questions to her about the size of the farm, the number of employees she had, and so on. They maintained this somewhat distant exchange until they had cleared the table and stacked the dishes for another absentee, a "daily" named Gretchen, to deal with in the morning.

For the rest of the evening they sat in the same room, Grethe explaining that as she had little leisure all day, she thought it extravagant to light a fire in the *zitkamer* just for the evening. Somehow her tone conveyed a criticism of those who had time enough on their hands to use a sitting-room at any earlier hour.

Again they talked commonplaces until Grethe sat more upright and appeared to brace herself for a task.

"We have not spoken of your father," she announced.

"No."

"And we must – though perhaps only once in this vein, and then not again. You know of course that as a young man he abandoned the farm and never came back to it, even when our brother Hans died, leaving only myself and Letti to maintain it? And Letti then was only a schoolgirl."

Jonnet admitted, "Yes, I knew, and that you were estranged because he stayed in England and did not come back. But was he so much to blame? He was mechanically

28

minded, a fine engineer, and he didn't want to grow bulbs for a living. Besides, I think he had only just married my mother, an English girl, and he had grown used to English life."

Grethe scorned, "An engineer! As if any good farm isn't motorized to a certain degree! He could have found scope enough for those talents, if he had cared to try. Instead — what? After one short return, when Dirk and you were no more than babes, he cut himself off from us, his family, and the living things we had been growing for generations of Handels, leaving me, a woman, to stand in for him and carry on. Which was not right by me or the property, as he must have known."

"Though hadn't you been doing it very well ever since our uncle Hans had died? Five years or so by then, wasn't it?" Jonnet enquired.

Grethe's chin went up. "Of course. Who else? Letti, the inept creature, never showed talent for anything other than getting herself married and widowed from time to time, and I had no one but Munt, who had come to us as a boy in your grandfather's time. But I would willingly have handed over to a man, had there been one in line. As it was, there was no one, nor has there been since, though the Boerdery Handel goes on — and will." She paused, then seemed to brace herself anew to continue, "But this said and understood, that is enough. I shall not reproach you with it again. Perhaps through no fault of your own, Dirk and you came late enough to Holland, but you are here now, and no doubt the future will arrange itself."

Jonnet was silent, working out the implications of this. It almost sounded as if —! She watched her aunt reach for a knitting-bag, producing from it the unfinished twin, in colour and shape, to the jumper she was wearing. Disposing wool and needles to her satisfaction, she began to knit,

29

while Jonnet sought balloon-pricking words which wouldn't sound too offensive – if, indeed, as she suspected, there were a balloon to be pricked.

At last she said, "Yes, and it is good of you to welcome us without any bitterness, Tante Grethe. But Dirk is only on a teaching job here. I can't think he has given you to understand that he means to stay permanently in Holland."

"No? He is a language teacher, is he not?"

"A teacher of English, yes."

"And he speaks Dutch perfectly, so why should he not choose to stay in Holland? Moving from school to school, perhaps, But there are many which would welcome him. Yes, I think he may stay. And if he does, no doubt he will marry ... have children who will be Handels. And so we shall see."

Jonnet conceded, "Well, I know he likes this country. He said so enthusiastically today. But he has never suggested staying here for good. And I –"

"You too," Grethe cut in briskly. "Should you do the same and choose one of our men, of course your children would not be Handels. But they would be born here of a Dutch father, and the family links need not suffer."

This was ridiculous! Momentarily nonplussed by this cloud-cuckoo disposal of Dirk's and her own future, Jonnet could find nothing to say which would not be over-brutally frank. At last she managed the mild protest of, "Isn't that looking a lot too far ahead, Tante Grethe? Don't forget that Dirk hasn't been here six months yet, and I've only just arrived!"

"Ah, true, true," Grethe nodded over her knitting. "And you, who haven't been brought up alongside growing things, can't understand the outlook of those of us who have. You think only for today. We – always of tomorrow.

For instance –" dropping her work in her lap and surveying Jonnet over her down-drawn spectacles – "consider the
seed that needs five years from bulblet to flower, or the new
strain that may take from fifteen years to a generation to
develop, and even then may not break 'true'. You wonder
then that we old ones have to *think* in terms of the generations ahead if the craft we have given our lives to is to
survive?"

"Yes, I see –" Rebuked and aware that she deserved it,
Jonnet began slowly, only to be cut short again by her
aunt's blunt, "I doubt if you do. But it is not to be expected. It is only with time that you will learn." Which, assuming as it did that she had limitless time for the lesson
and that she was yearning to learn it, left Jonnet feeling
trapped. Kindly trapped. Tolerantly trapped. But still –
trapped.

When, a little later, Grethe re-bagged her knitting,
looked at the mantelpiece clock and said that she kept early
hours at night, Jonnet was only too glad to escape to the
refuge of her room.

They said their good nights, Grethe adding, "We breakfast at eight. You eat a proper breakfast, I hope?"

Jonnet said she did, and they parted company. But before she had begun to undress, Grethe was at her door,
bearing a tin tray of an assortment of potted plants –
cineraria, a busy lizzie, a clump of polyanthus and a cactus
– which she proceeded to set out on the windowsill. "Your
flowers," she said. "I took them down to water and forgot
to return them. After this you will be able to tend them
yourself. But you have drawn your curtains, child!" Flinging them open again, "This we rarely do in Holland. We
are pleased that people should see the inside of our homes.
Not that there is anyone to overlook us here. But we like
our plants to get the morning light too –"

And that *is* about the end! thought Jonnet bleakly when she had gone. No privacy to be had or wanted, and pot-plants on a bedroom windowsill! It summed up all that was alien that had happened to her today, and suddenly feeling childishly forlorn, she wanted to cry.

She woke as the winter dawn was breaking and was surprised to find she felt less depressed. Overnight she had defiantly closed the curtain again, but now she got out of bed and went to open them on the scene outside.

Brown earth and sky; no hedges; the fields bordered and traversed by irrigation channels; the dim shape of a windmill in the middle distance. At least the wind seemed to have dropped, and there was a breaking of the cloud low down on the horizon.

Standing there as the light strengthened, Jonnet wondered what went on on a bulb farm in January unless flowers were being forced for the early market under glass, of which Grethe had told her she had none. As was more general in Holland than in the English bulb-growing regions, her main business was in bulbs as bulbs for sale. It was news which Jonnet hadn't expected, and her sentimentality resented the picture of acres of flower being de-headed in their prime for the better growth of the bulb. "If I were a tulip, I just wouldn't bother to bloom", she thought now, and for a time dreamily pursued the fantasy of a Trade Union of Spring Flowers which would go on strike against the outrage of being ruthlessly cut off in the fullness of their youth.

Glass. That reminded her of Axel Keyser's telling her to look for his own estate buildings to the right of the road. Being at the front of the house, she was facing the opposite way now, so she craned out of the window to the left. She could see the outline of them now – some glass and buildings which looked like offices, as well as sheds and store-houses.

Evidently he was in a bigger way of business than the Boerdery Handel. But of course he must be. That magnificent house on The Herengracht bore it out.

Entertained a lot, did he? Whooped it up? Went often to England? Her resentment of his interference in her affairs would have liked to see him as a kind of absentee landlord, taking only a money-grubbing interest in the estate. But from what he had said about his frequent commuting to it from the city, it looked as if he took an active hand in its management. Rather a pity, that, if it were so. She needed something to fan the flames of her justified rancour against him.

By the time she had dressed the break in the cloud had widened, showing blue sky, and there was some activity outside; the handful of men who had straggled up the road on bicycles, were now setting out across the fields with spraying-cans strapped to their backs and spray-guns in their hands.

Breakfast was a substantial meal of tea and hard-boiled eggs, cold sausage, nutty-tasting dark bread, butter and honey. "We take only *koffietafel* – something very light – at midday and eat more heavily again in the evening," Grethe said as warning that Jonnet should expect to bring a good appetite to breakfast. While they ate Jonnet put the question she had asked herself earlier and was told by Grethe,

"There is always plenty to do, all the year round. Just now we are spraying against weeds before the bulb crowns break soil. On wet days we clear the storehouses, make and mend the storing boxes, and for me there is always the paper work – the bills, the accounts, the letters. Munt directs the men and the seasonal women we take on for the gathering and at de-heading time, but I oversee everything. A business is like a ship – there must be someone in command."

They had finished eating and Jonnet was wondering what would be expected of her next when the telephone rang and Grethe, answering it, told her that it was Dirk on the line, wanting to speak to her. "Something about a bicycle," Grethe reported. Jonnet went to the phone.

"Axel told me last night he had persuaded you to stay." Dirk sounded relieved. "I asked him how, and he said 'Easy'. But whether or not, I'm glad, Jon – and grateful. So now, what about this bike? I've got a free afternoon, so I propose to come out to bring you in to the city, and you can choose one. My treat. O.K.?"

"O.K. But you don't have to give it to me. I can afford one myself," Jonnet told him.

"No, I'd like to make you a present of it. See you –" Dirk said, and rang off, leaving Jonnet's smouldering ire to feed upon "Easy". Easy, indeed! Why, she hadn't even told the man in so many words that she had decided to stay! She had, as it were, just left it on the table, and so had he. She supposed it was sheer male conceit that had needed to assure Dirk, man to man, that his persuasion of her had been "easy".

After breakfast Grethe went to the small room she used as an office, without assigning any task to Jonnet, nor making any suggestion as to how she should spend the morning. Left to herself, Jonnet looked into the other downstair rooms, dismissing the *zitkamer* as "pretty grim", and made the acquaintance of the shy Gretchen in the kitchen, a large light place, with an even lighter and cooler dairy opening off it.

To Gretchen she appealed for something to do, and after giving some thought to the matter, Gretchen deputed her to water the collection of pot plants which seemed to occupy the windowsills of every room in the house. Then, since

Gretchen proved barren of any further ideas, she put on her coat and went out from the back of the house to explore the yard and the outbuildings and the garden if there was one.

There wasn't – not, that is, as she understood the word. But Grethe did have some glass – a small greenhouse surrounded by a narrow border where snowdrops and the tip of some crocus spikes were showing through.

The door was ajar and the giant of a man who was working inside looked up as Jonnet approached. His weather-beaten face was framed by grizzled whiskers; he wore a thick leather apron, his shirt-sleeves were rolled to the elbow, and with fingers the size of fat sausages he was deftly sifting soil or peat into pots. Evidently the greenhouse was the supply depot for the house plants, for the stages were full of them and of cuttings, each one labelled.

Deciding he must be Grethe's manager, Jonnet began in Dutch, "You are Mijnheer Munt, I expect? I am Jonnet Handel. I arrived last –" She didn't finish, for he cut her short with a grunt.

"*Wel!* Another of them from England! What do you want?" he demanded.

Jonnet mistook his meaning. "Why, nothing," she hesitated. "My aunt was busy, so I was just looking round. I –" Her voice trailed away before his hostile glare.

"*Ach!*" He addressed the pot he was filling. "First the boy, now you. What do you want of the Boerdery Handel – either of you, or both?"

"Of the farm? *Want* of it? What do you mean?" Jonnet asked, though from his manner she thought she could guess. But how *dared* he?

He changed his question, "Of Grethe Handel, then? He comes. You come. Why?" then answered it himself, "Because you want something, of course! You come with your

35

eyes open and your hands out. Or *he* does. You – perhaps you only come to hang out your broom in our country, having had no success at it in your own. Bah, you may think no one sees what you are about. But *I* do. Make no mistake about that, *me juffrouw!*"

With as much dignity as she could summon Jonnet said, "You make it very clear that you think you know. But you don't. Neither Dirk nor I have our hands out, wanting anything of our aunt for ourselves. *He* decided to move into Amsterdam, so I came instead to stay with her for a while. That is all. And as for hanging out my broom, I simply don't know what you mean!"

He put aside one pot, began to fill another. "You speak our language well. I think you do," he growled.

"I don't. What *did* you mean?" she pressed, then gave up and turned away. "Or no, don't bother. It doesn't matter," she added over her shoulder as she left him, her indignation near the boil and her mind full of questions.

No particular welcome from Tante Grethe, and hostility like this in the background! How *was* she going to cope? Had Munt vented his doubts of their motives on Dirk too? If so, why hadn't Dirk warned her? Did Tante Grethe know? Meanwhile, she had a pressing need of a Dutch-English dictionary and fortunately had brought her own with her. It was a good one, giving simple phrases of the use of a word as well as its meaning. So that with luck, by looking up *de bezem* for "Broom" –?

Luck was with her. In her room she dragged the volume from the bottom of her suitcase, frenziedly leafed through it to the page she wanted, and the word. She ran a hasty finger down the samples given. Yes, it was there. *Ze hangt de bezem uit*. But its English meaning! Incredulous, she mouthed it aloud and clapped shut the dictionary with a long-drawn, "Well!" of chagrin.

36

She spent the rest of the morning settling into her room and writing to the friends with whom she had been staying before coming over, a cautious letter of her first impressions. Before she joined Grethe for their snack of coffee and cheese and biscuits she had already decided to tone down Munt's reception of her. She would keep its full acrimony for reporting to Dirk. And so, when Grethe asked if she had come across Munt during the morning, she only said, "Yes. He was in your greenhouse, so I introduced myself. I didn't stay long with him. He seemed busy and he was a bit – terse."

"Ah, that is his way." Grethe didn't sound surprised. "He does not care for strangers and regards himself as my watchdog and the farm as good as his own. He gets above himself, that one. But we understand each other, he and I. He loves bulbs more than he likes people, that is all," she finished comfortably.

I'll say he gets above himself! Jonnet thought as she waited for Dirk to come for her. When he did and wanted to hear about her first evening and morning, she gave him a blow-by-blow account of them in full detail.

"Did you realise that Tante Grethe has already decided you are a permanency here?" she accused him.

"M'm," he agreed. "She had hinted as much."

"Was that why you decided to get out from under?"

"Good heavens, no. I wanted to live in the city for the reasons I've told you. Anyway, there's no harm in her hoping. Had she got any plans for *you*?"

"Much the same as for you. She'll have us both married to Dutch partners, if we don't watch out."

"So? Well, we might do worse at that."

Jonnet's jaw dropped. "You mean you'd *consider* it? Have done already, perhaps?"

"Not really. There hasn't been time. But Mother mar-

37

ried Father and found she liked it," he reminded her. "Anyway, what about Munt? How have you got on with him?"

"I haven't," Jonnet snapped. "I came upon him in the greenhouse and he let fly almost at once. What do you think he accused me of – and you too? Of our coming over with an eye to the main chance; with designs on the farm – inheriting it, or even trying to grab it now, I wouldn't be surprised –"

"Nonsense. He couldn't be serious," Dirk soothed.

"No? You didn't hear him. And that wasn't all," Jonnet declared, warming to her theme. "He taunted *me* with coming to Holland to hang out my broom –"

At that Dirk chortled with laughter. "Oh, *poor* Jon! He said that, and you understood him?"

"Not then. I'm glad I didn't, for I'd have been tempted to throttle the man. I had to look it up in the dictionary, and there it was under '*bezem – Ze hangt de bezem uit* – She is looking for a husband.' Me! I ask you! When I didn't want to come over here at all!"

Infuriatingly, Dirk laughed again and repeated, "Poor Jon, you did buy it, didn't you? But you mustn't be so thin-skinned. *You* know you aren't on the make for either a bulb-farm or a husband, so what?"

"It doesn't matter, I suppose, that I'm expected to live cheek-by-jowl with someone who thinks I am?"

"I doubt if Munt does. He was just blowing his top. I've heard him. And 'cheek-by-jowl' doesn't apply. Munt practically lives the life of a hermit – in the place, but not often of it, if you see what I mean?"

"Well, thank goodness for that, if it's true. Why, what is it?" They were into the city now and her question was occasioned by Dirk's slowing down and signalling to someone – a girl – on the sidewalk. She signalled back. Dirk stopped the car and she came over.

She was a petite creature, hatless with black centre-parted hair caught back behind her ears. Everything about her was in miniature, from her slender figure in a black-and-white trouser suit to her piquant heart-shaped face and to the tiny gloved hand which she rested on Dirk's wound-down window.

"Why, Dirk," she said in Dutch. And looking beyond him, "And this is –?"

"Yes. Jonnet. She arrived yesterday. Jonnet, meet Saskia, Tante Letti's stepdaughter." He added to Saskia, "I can't stop here. Get in, and make Jonnet's acquaintance, and I'll drop you wherever you were going."

"Oh, sweet of you." Her smile was dimpled. As she joined them – "In fact, I was only going window-shopping on the Kalverstraat. Where are you going yourselves?"

"To buy Jonnet a bicycle. Come along with us and then back to my flat. Where do you recommend?"

"For a *bicycle*?" Saskia puckered delicate brows over the word, as she might have done over "hobby-horse" or "velocipede". "My dear Dirk, I don't know where." She turned to Jonnet. "What do you want one for? Don't you drive?"

"No. And if I did, I haven't a car. Have you?" Jonnet asked.

"Of my own? Oh yes, and I thought everyone drove nowadays. How odd of you not to, unless you've got a man of your own to do it for you!" To Dirk Saskia added, "I'd love to go back to your place. And where after that? I'm free."

"I shan't be for very long. I shall have to take Jonnet back, plus bicycle if she gets one," Dirk said.

"Oh. I'd hoped we might –" Saskia drew down the corners of her rosebud mouth and asked Jonnet, "If you do buy one, aren't you going to ride it? I'd have thought you would want to."

Until that moment Jonnet had had no intention of negotiating the return journey to the farm on a strange machine, hampered as she would be by the Continental rule of the road which was new to her. But she was irritated by the hint of patronage which sounded in almost every word the other girl had uttered, so she said, "Of course I mean to ride it. What else?" and to Dirk's murmured protest, snapped, "Nonsense. I've ridden across London in the rush hour before now. So what's Amsterdam, compared with that?"

"It's strange to you," said Dirk dryly. "And you have sixteen or so kilometres to go beyond it."

"With the wind behind me, on a road as flat and dull as a – a pastry-board."

"And by the time you get going the light may be failing."

"I suppose even Dutch pushbikes run to lamps?"

"And if she *wants* to?" pleaded Saskia, an ally with whose help Jonnet could have dispensed.

Dirk said, "Over my dead body!" But when, after trying several bicycles at the store they visited, Jonnet was suited with one she liked very much and pointed out that if she were going to use it for coming into the city alone, she might as well learn the way in and out at once, he reluctantly gave in, on condition that she left well before dark.

Not particularly relishing Saskia's company for the rest of the afternoon, "I'll go straight away, if you like," Jonnet offered.

But to that Dirk said, "No. We'll leave the thing here, and I'll drive you to pick it up. Because, though Axel is out, he said I could show you over the house, and I'd like you to see to it. It's rather fine."

Overhearing that Axel was to be out, Saskia pouted, "Oh, won't he be there? Have you met Axel Keyser yet?

But you only arrived yesterday, so probably you haven't?" she asked Jonnet.

Jonnet said, "In fact I have. We came over by the same plane, and as Dirk couldn't take me out to the farm, he did. You know him too, do you?"

Saskia's eyes widened. "But of course! Everyone in our circle in Amsterdam knows Axel! He positively mows the girls down. And he calls me his little *katje*, doesn't he, Dirk?"

Which was how Dirk himself had described her – as a dishy kitten, Jonnet remembered. As indeed she was – slinky and appealing and all-velvet, though with secret claws. Or was that too hasty a measurement of her surface charm? Perhaps. But Jonnet had a feeling that Saskia Moet was not going to become one of her favourite people.

Her impression that Saskia would like to be tête-à-tête with Dirk was strengthened when, after they had had tea in his flat, Saskia wondered aloud whether it wasn't time that Jonnet was on her way. It got dark so *very* early this month –

But Dirk hadn't yet shown Jonnet Axel's house, and wanted to. Saskia came with them, and as he unlocked the connecting door, Jonnet asked her what they planned to do after she had left. Saskia said, "Well, I'd thought a film would be nice, and afterwards I'd take Dirk home and I'd ring up some people and we'd dance or something . . . have a party. Shall we do that, Dirk?"

"Fine," he agreed, and Saskia added graciously to Jonnet, "You must come and meet Letti some time. I'll get her to ring you up."

"Letti?" Jonnet echoed, for the moment at a loss.

"Oh yes." Saskia laughed softly. "She is not my mother, you see, so I call her Letti and she likes it. She says it makes her feel like an elder sister to me. Your aunt Grethe disapproves, but she disapproves of so much that one can't keep pace."

The house was enormous. From front to back it ran the depth of the block, the back giving on to the street behind it. The reception rooms were on the floor above Dirk's flat; the salon gave on to a *serre*, a back balcony railed about by intricate wrought-iron beyond the floor-to-ceiling windows. Behind the dining-room were some smaller rooms and the kitchen quarters. The typically steep staircase led up to the bedrooms and Axel's study on the floor above; there were more rooms above that, and attics on the floor of the topmost gable. From the back windows of each of the upper levels there was an increasingly good view of the wide waters of the Ijsselmeer. Up there it was extraordinarily peaceful; the racket of the street sounds below were muted; the house might not have been a town mansion at the very heart of a city at all.

The furnishing was expectedly in keeping – rich curtaining and much dark oak, dressers set out with the blue-and-white of priceless old Delft ware and cabinets filled with gleaming silver. Only the study was modern and functional, with a leather-topped desk, leather chairs and shelves of technical books. Here Saskia sat at the desk, shifted the position of the telephone, drew the blotter towards her and riffled through the pages of a city directory.

"I'm Axel, playing at being an executive type," she announced with a giggle. "As if he need, with all *his* money! Letti teases him that he ought to get married; says it's a shame for a house like this to be running to waste without a mistress."

Dirk said mildly, "It has never struck me as coming to much harm. I daresay he feels he has time on his side – he's not much over thirty, and goodness knows he'll probably have plenty of choice."

42

Saskia wrinkled her nose at him. "Spoken just like a man," she taunted. "Can you never admit that it's the girl who sets the pace more often than not? For instance, supposing *I* decided to make a bid for Axel, do you suppose I couldn't win?"

As she put the coy question Jonnet, who was watching Dirk, was surprised at the shadow which crossed his face. He said obliquely, "From what you say, Tante Letti would probably be gratified if you did."

Saskia's little gesture made nothing of her stepmother's opinion. "I'm asking *you*," she urged. But she got no satisfaction from Dirk. "It would be nothing to do with me," he said shortly as he moved out of the room, leaving the girls to follow. All the same, his reluctance to discuss Saskia's suggestion of her making a play for Axel's attention left Jonnet vaguely disturbed. Surely he wasn't falling for Saskia himself? *Surely* not?

When she parted from them at the bicycle shop Jonnet set out jauntily enough, reluctant to let Saskia guess that she saw the ride through Amsterdam's crowded streets as something of an adventure. Fortunately it was not the full rush hour, but the cycle traffic was in strong competition with the cars and trams, and at every set of traffic lights the halted bicycles lined up six and seven abreast.

Many of the cyclists were children out of school, and Jonnet was puzzled by the luminous-painted satchels or saddle-bags which many of them carried, until she realised they were cautionary devices against the riders' being run down in bad light.

She found she was less bothered than she had expected by the Keep Right rule of the road; the stream of traffic going her way made it comparatively easy to follow, and besides the implicit directions which Dirk had given her, she had noted various landmarks on the way in and came upon them again without much difficulty. The level going was so easy that she was out into the suburbs and then on to the open road at better speed than she had hoped to make. But the winter afternoon had darkened quickly and though it was not yet lighting-up time, in common with most of the other road users she switched on her lamps. The air was cold, promising frost, but it was still fairly windless and she found she was enjoying herself unreservedly for the first time since she had arrived.

She calculated she was about eight kilometres from the farm when the beam of her front lamp caught something bright on the grass verge – a colour recently seen and remembered. Of course! It was the garish, luminous orange of the schoolchildren's satchels. But – *down there*? Instead of just above saddle-level? That meant –! She was off her own machine with a leap, flinging it on to the verge as she reached for the orange bag and saw why it was there; saw the grotesquely twisted bicycle and the huddle of clothes and limbs that was the child who had lately ridden it. Both were hidden from the road by the slope downward from the verge; both must have been struck with force for them to have been flung so far.

Jonnet snatched her lamp from its bracket and flopped beside the child. She found she was kneeling in a runnel of water and the little girl was lying in it. She was whimpering and she was conscious, but Jonnet dared not move her, lest she do more harm than good. She spoke soothingly in Dutch and taking off her coat, laid it blanketwise over the child. Then, raging inwardly against the hit-and-run driver who must have been responsible, she returned to the verge to flag down any oncoming car.

Having left the lamp by the child, she was signalling by hand, and when two cars had ignored her and swept by, she realised the drivers thought she was merely thumbing a lift, and was about to wave the red of her rear-lamp when she realised a third car was slowing and stopping. It drew up alongside, and before she could dash to the driver's lowered window, he was out of the car and taking her forcibly by her coatless shoulders.

He was Axel Keyser. He uttered an expletive and stared down at her, his eyes angry. "Jonnet Handel! What do you think you're doing?" he demanded. "Dirk said he was bringing you into town to buy you a bicycle, but what did he mean by letting you out on it alone for the first time and after dark?"

Jonnet protested, "He didn't 'let' me. I wanted to ride it –"

"Coatless and hatless – in *this* temperature!"

"I'm *not*. I have a coat. And you've got it all wrong–"

"That you were flagging me down because you've run into trouble – wrong?"

"I wasn't flagging you. I was flagging any car that would stop. Yours was the first that did. Oh, *listen*, will you?" In her panic she grabbed at his lapels and shook them. "I'm *not* in trouble. But someone is – a schoolgirl whom some speed-hog was knocked off her bike. She's down here. Look! I found her a few minutes ago. I haven't tried to move her, nor done anything for her, just covered her with my coat. *That* mess is her bicycle," she added, pointing towards it.

Axel knelt by the child and after removing Jonnet's coat and handing it back, examined the cut face and the torn hands and gently moved each arm and leg. "I think we can afford to move her," he told Jonnet, taking off his own top coat and wrapping the child in it. On the way to his car he said, "I know her," and looking down, "Don't I, Lysbet?"

She nodded dumbly, and he explained, "Her father, Franz Bernard, works for me. She would have been on her

45

way home from school."

"I know," said Jonnet. "They were all coming through the city at the same time as I was – Oh!"

"What?" Axel looked at her.

"I've just remembered what probably happened. A few minutes before I came on her, a car raced past me at a wicked speed. It was so close that it would have caught my handlebars if I'd turned them a fraction. I should think it was that one that hit and ran."

"So that this –" indicating his burden – "might have been you?"

"I suppose so," she allowed, "though I'm pretty experienced."

"Experience doesn't always count." He made Lysbet comfortable on the seat beside his and loaded the broken bicycle into the back of the estate car he was driving today. "Now yours and you," he told Jonnet.

But she was already retrieving her machine from the verge. "No, I'm riding the rest of the way," she said.

"You're doing no such thing."

"Of course I am. Look," she argued, "if you're taking Lysbet home, you might later have to take her to a doctor or even to hospital, and you don't want to be hampered with me."

"In any event like that I shouldn't consider you overmuch. I'd see you safe when it suited me and not a minute before. However, you make your point and I don't insist. You can have your own way – this time." He slammed shut the back doors of the car, took the driving-seat and looked up at her through the lowered window.

"Only don't think, Jonnet Handel," he warned, "that in anything big which really matters you can always be the immovable object of the legend."

On her saddle, ready to move off, she frowned down at

46

him. "What do you mean? What immovable object?" she demanded.

"Why, the one that met the irresistible force. Their collision made for the most hideous deadlock of all time – remember?" he invited with a disarming smile which should have taken the sting from the words but didn't.

He waited for her to ride away first, then passed her and gathered speed.

CHAPTER THREE

THE next morning the low cloud was back again, dispelling all Jonnet's exhilaration on her bicycle ride. What was she supposed to do with her time? she wondered. Her aunt showed no pressing need of her company, Gretchen seemed self-sufficient in the kitchen, and she thought it discreet to keep clear of Mijnheer Munt. When she had been at work and later had cared for her father at home, she had always been busy, and idleness irked her. Here it had been all very well for Dirk; he had driven away to his own job every day. She felt she must find out what help or companionship Grethe had envisaged from her stay, and do what she could to comply, if only to prove (prove to whom?) that having set her hand to the plough, she wasn't drawing back.

Meanwhile she was anxious about little Lysbet Bernard and wished she had asked Axel Keyser to telephone her with news of the child. Consulted, Grethe suggested telephoning him at his office on the estate where he might be shortly, and Jonnet decided she must risk more smart-alec quips at her expense by doing so.

Questioned on the matter of occupation for her niece, Grethe was vaguely unhelpful. "Dirk said he wanted to give you a long holiday and a chance to know our country. I doubt whether you have any skills that I can use until you have learned more about our ways over here," she demurred.

Stung, Jonnet pointed out that since her mother's death she had both held down a job and kept house for her father and Dirk while the latter was at college. Grethe was unimpressed.

"Ah, an *English* house. But I am mistress here in my own, and I have Gretchen and Munt to help me," she disparaged.

"Perhaps I could do some shopping for you?" Jonnet suggested.

"That would not take much of your time. Now and again in the village, perhaps. But we do our own baking, we have delivery merchants and Munt fetches other stores from the city."

"On the farm, then?" Jonnet tried again. "While I'm here I ought to learn something about bulb-growing, don't you think?"

"Later . . . later, perhaps. There is little but men's heavy work to be done now. The bulbs are still asleep in the soil. But two months . . . three . . . in the season – yes, then any extra pair of hands is welcome," Grethe allowed.

(Though don't count your chickens. Three months of this existence and I could have expired of boredom) was Jonnet's mental comment on that. Aloud she made a last effort. "Then perhaps in your office, Tante Grethe? Couldn't I help you with some clerical work there?"

It was the first suggestion Grethe hadn't brushed aside with despatch. "You mean by typewriter. But I haven't one," she said slowly.

Not without irony Jonnet said, "Well, I can *write*," and was encouraged by her aunt's thoughtful nod. "Yes, well – perhaps," she said. "There are letters, accounts, orders – if you know anything of such things and have enough Dutch, you may be able to deal with them for me. Forms in duplicate, licences to grow this, that, how much of it and where; crop returns to the Ministry, claims –" She cut short the catalogue of onerous paperwork to allow herself a crinkled-pippin smile. "A secretary! 'Grethe Handel has a secretary. She gets above herself!' people will say of me in the markets. But no matter. It is only that they will envy me, wishing they had one themselves!"

Jonnet returned the smile, warming to it and to the touch of impish humour of which she hadn't thought Grethe capable. The small victory she had gained was welcome too, and after she had made her telephone call she joined Grethe in her office.

She had had to run the gauntlet of a telephone clerk and a secretary to reach Axel, who said he was glad she had called, though he hadn't afforded her much of his time nor, this time, found anything caustic to say. The doctor, he told her, had said Lysbet was very lucky, in that she had suffered nothing more serious than a degree of shock and some cuts and bruises. She would be away from school for somedays, and he suggested that Jonnet might like to go to see her in a few days' time.

"I'll do that," Jonnet agreed. "Where does she live?"

He had directed her, told her it was an easy bicycle ride, and had rung off. He hadn't made any further suggestion about showing her his estate, and as she replaced the receiver she had wondered why she felt disappointed. It certainly couldn't be that she craved the company of a man who openly despised her for her prejudices and her independence of him. So it had to be that her fighting spirit half enjoyed crossing swords with his assumptions of his right to judge her on the practically nothing he knew of her. He had jumped to too many conclusions from her few unguarded remarks, and though so far he had won, it should take only one or two more telling sessions with him to prove him wrong. But opportunity was a fine thing, and if it were to be denied her, *that* was why she felt cheated by his silence. Just that. Only that.

During that first morning with the farm's paperwork, she gave Grethe full marks for patience with her bewildered questions on the intricacies of Dutch invoices and general accounts. It was something, she supposed, that Grethe's own system seemed to be of the most primitive nature, consisting as it did of some large cash books, one letter tray marked "In" and another, "Pending" – the function of neither being fulfilled very accurately this morning; a filing system of some old-fashioned spikes for the pinioning of bills and receipts, and a petty cash till which, as Jonnet was to find later, was apt to be raided and I.O.U.'d by Munt, Gretchen and Grethe herself in the quest for household small change.

Practical and efficient bulb-grower of long standing Grethe might be. But she was no office organiser, and in consequence Jonnet felt that her own methods could hardly prove to be worse. What was more, her aunt seemed willing to give her reasonable rein in making some changes, one of her few conditions being that Munt should be made as free of the petty cash as always. "The foolish man never seems to carry any ready money for tobacco or bootlaces. But he always pays back what he owes, so what matter?" was her tolerant comment.

During those initial days on the farm Jonnet decided that their long years in harness must have acclimatised Grethe to her manager's frequent truculence and opposition to her orders, for though even in her first week Jonnet was witness to more than one acrimonious exchange between them, they never remained at loggerheads for long, a circumstance which she envied them, wondering idly how long it really took to learn to accept hard-hitting criticism from someone, and still keep them as a friend . . .

One such altercation was occasioned by Munt's storming into the office one morning to demand why the protective winter covering of strewn peat and straw was to be removed from one of the fields.

"I thought it time it came off," Grethe told him.

51

"Woman, it is still January! Can you not read your calendar?"

"Indeed I can. Very soon now the crop will be breaking soil, and the bulbs must breathe."

"Breathe an air that can yet drop well below zero, as you should know. And the Laag Veld collecting all the frost there is!"

"Yes. Very well, leave the stuff on the Laag Veld, and clear it from the rest."

"It will come off *them* in the first week in February, and from the Laag Veld when I see fit, not before. And if you don't like that, then you'd better get yourself another manager," Munt defied, and subjected his mistress to a long, hostile stare before stumping out.

To Jonnet's surprise Grethe seemed unmoved. "He doesn't mean that," she said. "He wouldn't for the world miss telling me 'I told you so' if I insist on the cover coming off and we have deep frost after the crowns come through. And I shan't miss saying it to him if it is left in place and we have no frost. In that way we both have a chance to win, and all becomes *gezellig* between us once more."

Gezellig. Cosy. It was a word, Jonnet was to learn, much favoured by the Dutch to describe anything or anyone they found charming, intimate, friendly. But spoken of the climate existing between Grethe and Munt, it sounded out of place. "Temperature uncertain" would be more applicable, she thought, and found she was again making comparisons. For hadn't she incurred something like it herself? Not that, in her relationship with Axel Keyser, was cosiness likely to be either offered or sought. *That,* up to date, had been just a wary circling of two people's opposing wills, with nothing but surface emotion involved.

On the day, a little later, when Jonnet proposed to visit

Lysbet Bernard, another difference arose between Grethe and her manager.

Grethe had suggested that Jonnet must take flowers to the child and went with her to the greenhouse to choose a plant. Munt turned a grudging eye on the one Jonnet selected – a pot of African violets in a rich shade of pink. "It is my best specimen," he grumbled.

"Yes. That is why we chose it," Grethe told him.

"What do you want with it?"

"To give to a sick child. What better purpose?"

"That one was for the house. There are others which would serve equally well."

"Then they can serve the house and the child shall have this one," Grethe insisted, brushing aside Jonnet's peacemaking suggestions that she could easily choose something else. The pot was borne away to be wrapped in white paper against damage by the wind, and Grethe, not at all put out, remarked comfortably, "It is as I told you. Munt prefers his flowers to people and is apt to forget his charity, even to sick ones."

The afternoon was one of sharp wind-frost which stung even booted toes, gloved fingertips and whipped painfully at cheeks, and Jonnet was glad to reach the small huddle of cottages, one of which was Lysbet's home. She was welcomed into the warm overcrowded living room by an old lady dressed as nearly in Dutch folk-costume as Jonnet had yet seen – a dark green ankle-length dress, heavily braided at its deep square neck, worn over a puffed-sleeve blouse and with a bunny-eared white cap. She was Lysbet's grandmother, she explained. The child had no mother, only a father.

Lysbet was busy with a jigsaw puzzle. She seemed pleased to see Jonnet, was delighted with the flowers, Jonnet was praised for her command of Dutch, and Grandmother Bernard was pressing with invitations to coffee, to tea, to an *advocaat* or at least to *koekjes*. Jonnet accepted a biscuit, but refused anything else, saying she had just taken *koffietafel*, and the three of them sat chatting until there was a knock at the door, its handle turned, and Axel Keyser looked round it.

The old lady bustled to greet him. "Mijnheer Keyser! *Two* welcome visitors to us! You see here Mejuffrouw Handel, who –"

"Yes." He nodded to Jonnet and tweaked Lysbet's hair. Jonnet realised that her look of surprise at seeing him may have appeared like eagerness to do so. "I didn't hear your car," she told him.

"I didn't bring it. I cycled over."

"Cycled?"

"In order to accompany you back." He was hauling a box of chocolates from a pocket, passing them to Lysbet. Her eyes sparkled. "Oh, Mijnheer!" He went on to Jonnet, "I rang the farm, to hear that you had come to see Lysbet. If you remember, I'd told you I would show you my place, and I'd thought we might do that this afternoon, if you'd care to?"

She told herself she was proof against gratification that he had kept his promise. "Thank you. I'd like that," she told him politely.

"Then if Mevrouw Bernard will excuse you now, perhaps you could come again another day, before Lysbet goes back to school." He turned to the old lady. "You should know, *mevrouw*, that we have here a young woman who thought nothing that was good of Holland before she set foot in it, so we must lose no time in teaching her otherwise – h'm?"

Mevrouw Bernard turned shocked eyes upon Jonnet. "You do not like our country? But surely, *mejuffrouw*,

54

your family is Dutch! Your aunts, your father – and you yourself a Handel! You cannot mean that you are not happy with Holland? No! It is so beautiful, so open; its soil so rich, its air so clear, and its cities – elegant! And when you know us, we, its people, friendly ... *gezellig*. Yes, indeed you must learn this, *mejuffrouw*, indeed!"

Not for the first time Jonnet regretted her ill-tempered outburst which had brought down all this misjudgement and criticism on her head. Axel Keyser hadn't betrayed her to Dirk, which was something, she supposed. But evidently he didn't intend she should forget her folly while he could remind her of it in order to score a point.

She began to excuse herself. "I'm afraid I spoke a bit rashly in Mijnheer Keyser's overhearing –" but was cut short by his telling the old lady, "And *I* am afraid that *gezellig* is a word that Mejuffrouw Handel doesn't want to understand of us. Do you know, *mevrouw*, she thinks we do no work, indulge in no pleasures; instead we perch on the sails of our windmills, champing our cheeses and holding on to our hats against the wind – all of us, podgy burghers and worthy housewives alike?"

At that Lysbet set up a shout of laughter and her grandmother looked doubtful of her own hearing. "Oh no, *mijnheer*, this is nonsense which she cannot believe!" she protested.

Axel's clear blue eyes widened. "I do assure you!"

But the old lady shook her head. "No, you are joking, I can see."

He grinned. "Well, only a very little –"

"Yet still too much for your purpose, I think, *mijnheer*. You will not teach the *mejuffrouw* to love our country if you mock and make fun."

"You think not? Well, we shall see. But if not, I may have other methods in my pouch in reserve." Limbering

55

himself from the table-edge where he had perched, he changed the subject to tell them that the police had come up with the hit-and-run driver, who, in a stolen car, had caused a later collision and had admitted to Lysbet's accident, which Axel had reported. Then Jonnet took her leave, asking if she might come again, and they went out together.

He wheeled both bicycles out into the road and handed Jonnet's to her. "If I had known this morning that I could make time to escort you, I'd have worn my best clogs," he said.

She mounted and waited until he came abreast of her. "You don't give up easily, do you?" she asked.

"Not once I've taken the bit between my teeth."

"And that dark threat about your having other means of persuading me to love Holland, if sarcasm doesn't work. What did that mean?"

He shook his head. "Ah, that secret is my privilege. Not that I claim that when you leave, you will go, loving us – only that you'll go, knowing more about us, appreciating that we're not just a picture-postcard image and, I hope, being generous enough to admit you were wrong. And so, Lesson One in appreciation –" he indicated the wide landscape and the meeting sky before and around them – "can I get you to allow Mevrouw Bernard's claim that we are 'so open'?"

Jonnet looked about her. "No more so than Lincolnshire or the Fens," she said.

He grimaced. "Too early for results. What did I expect?"

"It's just that you make more of a song and dance about your breadth of countryside. We accept that ours is *there*."

His expression changed, turned graver. "No doubt because ours wasn't 'there' originally. Most of it we had to win from the sea, and to fight for something makes it precious. You've probably heard the saying 'God made the world; the Dutch made Holland'?"

"Yes."

"Good. However, as you can't be expected to appreciate the quality of our soil, what about Mevrouw Bernard's next point – the clarity of our air?"

Jonnet exhaled a long breath which lingered visibly. "It bites. And it shows."

"Well, wouldn't it in England at this date?" he parried. "But no good word for our cities either?"

"I've only seen Amsterdam, and I've never pretended to have anything against it."

He laughed shortly. "Damned with faint praise indeed!"

She flushed. "I didn't mean that. I do think it's beautiful. And I liked your house very much."

"You did? Fit domicile, you thought, for a podgy burgher to rattle about in?"

She turned on him at that. "Dirk had no right to report to you that I'd said you must rattle!"

"But it's your considered opinion that I must?"

"That was before I'd really seen it, and before I knew who you were. It was" – she bit her lip – "that first day."

"Of shaming memory, one trusts." As they approached the entrance to his estate, he added mock-soothingly, "All right. All Is Forgiven – or nearly. Meanwhile, here we are. Lesson Two coming up."

The double wrought-iron gates were open and they could have ridden through on to the curved sweep of drive beyond. But Jonnet put down a foot to balance herself and pointed up at the scrolled iron lettering which formed the archway. "I've passed here several times. I suppose that's the name of your estate – *Het Wijdellande*?"

"Yes. In English, roughly – The Broad Lands."

"It's on a much bigger scale than the Boerdery Handel?"

"A good deal now. But a couple of generations back it

57

was only a family concern, like yours. My grandfather and his father dug their own bulb-fields and took their produce to market in horse-drawn tumbrils." Axel rode on and they dismounted outside the long one-storied building which housed his offices.

It was a busy place. Behind glass-panelled doors typewriters clacked; the doors themselves opened and shut on people in earnest talk; the girls the two met in the corridors murmured *"Goeden dag, mijnheer,"* to Axel and eyed Jonnet with curious interest, and now and then a man would buttonhole Axel with a question. Axel's own office was a large light room where he introduced Jonnet to his secretary, Mevrouw Schoon, whom he asked to order tea for them, naming a time.

"You would like it in your room?"

"Please." His hand lightly at Jonnet's back, he propelled her out of the building, saying, "The rest now – the bulb storage barns and the glasshouses and the fields. Are you equal to walking for an hour, some of it rather rough going?"

At this season the storage sheds had little to show but the ranks of empty staging where the bulbs would come after their lifting in high summer. Axel outlined the cycle of forcing – the early autumn selection of bulbs for planting and watering in boxes, straw-covered to conserve heat and moisture; their being left out of doors for the development of a good root system and a strong embryo shoot, until their transfer to heat under glass and their gradual encouragement into flower, mainly for sale at the daily auction market at Aalsmeer. The field bulbs, he said, after lifting and drying in the open, would be replanted during any time between August and October.

"Tante Grethe grows more tulips than anything else, she says. Do you?" Jonnet asked.

"As our principal crop, yes. As do most growers in Holland. Daffodils are secondary, and for forcing. Iris and hyacinth in lesser quantities still, though hyacinths sell on the bulb's colour, and no soil in the world can deliver as rich a coloured bulb as ours does," Axel told her.

He took her next to his glasshouses where girls were gathering just opened, pencil-straight daffodil blooms and where other stagings held African violet plants, from tiny cuttings to fully-leaved blossoms, the latter in every conceivable shade from deepest purple to carmine. They made a sea of colour, at which Jonnet gasped in delight.

"They are a surprise," she said. "I'd understood from my aunt that Holland didn't go in for much glass?"

He agreed, "We used not to. But I'm one of the pioneers who didn't see why England and the Channel Islands should make a corner in glass. The initial investment is colossal, but in a trade where Mother Nature can be our worst enemy, it's a wise insurance in the bad years, and an extra bonus in the good."

As they went out to the fields Jonnet asked what hazards the industry had to face.

"Evidently I'm not wasting my time. You're showing an intelligent interest!" he mocked. "Well — frost, against which we can guard; disease which we can control with fungicides, and hail at blossom time, against which we can only pray. In my time I've seen three hectares — that's seven or eight acres — of tulips beheaded in a single day's storms."

"And flooding?"

"Not so much, now we've made a servant of water instead of the master it was for centuries. Here, by the way, I'm harnessing it for pleasure. I'll show you, before we go back."

It was nearly twilight by the time they had tramped the perimeters of the fields, the low-lying ones still blanketed against frost, some of the others showing enough growth for the predominating brown of the soil to be hazed over with green. Then, at some distance short of the boundary of Axel's land and sheltered by a thick belt of conifers, there was the water – a whole lake of it, its surface grey and wind-ruffled, its surrounding "beach" a gentle slope of shingle down to the lap-lap of the shallow water at its edge.

Here there were signs of a different kind of busyness – excavations being dug, piled loads of timber and a plantation of young trees and shrubs taking shape, bare flower-beds of dark rich tilth and autumn-sown young grass showing green on a levelled lawn.

Jonnet looked about her. "You are making a garden here – a kind of lake-garden," she said.

Axel nodded. "That's the idea – a rustic lido. Over there," he pointed towards the boundary, "there is access from a road, and I'm planning a miniature Keukenhof for people to visit. You've heard of the Keukenhof near Lisse, I daresay?"

"They are the exhibition flower-gardens, aren't they?"

"And more. Keukenhof is a research and conference centre too. You have something on the same lines in your Lincolnshire bulb country. But I don't aim so high – just a pleasant picnic-place, a swimming place, a model-boating place, a lovers' nook place, skating in winter – Do you skate?"

"No." On the defensive, Jonnet added, "I've had neither the time nor the chance to learn. In England –"

"I know. In England you get about one winter in twenty when the ice will bear. But you swim, I suppose?"

"Oh yes." She added drily, "I'm not a model-boat owner, though."

"Nor, currently, a lover in need of a nook?"

"Not at the moment."

60

"Well, let me know when you are, and we'll have a direction sign put up. However, do you approve of the scheme – gazebos, bathing cabins" – he gestured towards the waiting timber – "the lot?"

She nodded. "I like it, yes. When do you hope to open it to the public?"

"If we had hard frost, skating could go on now. The rest – by the early summer at latest. But 'open to the public' – what a municipal phrase! I mean this to be free to anyone who is passing and cares to look in."

"Free? But aren't people going to exploit you?"

He shrugged. "That remains to be seen, though I've a theory that if you expect to be cheated, you are. If not, not. With which maxim, I may say, your aunt doesn't hold. She calls this my Folly, and thinks me mad to turn hectares of good bulb land over to it, without making a profit."

Jonnet said slowly, "Well, it *is* generous of you." She met his glance. "What?" she asked of the amused glint in the blue eyes.

"I was thinking," he said, "that that's the first tolerant judgement of me I've heard you utter."

"Well, you haven't been over-free with tolerance yourself, have you?" she retorted.

"Ah, but I took on the task of showing you the error of your ways, and a teacher has the right to be critical. Besides, my estimate of you is that you are a Death or Glory type – you don't willingly pass up the chance of a scrap in which you hope you might win."

That was so shrewd a measurement of her sense of having been cheated when she thought he had finished with her that she flushed and knew he had noticed.

"In other words," she said, "you may sometimes have baited me deliberately, in order to keep our differences going?"

61

He shook his head. "That would be taking an unfair advantage. No, so far, without needing to prod you into controversy, I've found you to be an opponent well worthy of my steel." Upon which he put an arm into hers and kept it firmly there all the way back to the office building. *Making sure I shan't get away*, thought Jonnet of the arm's hard rigidity, which was more that of a grappling-iron than of an intimate gesture.

The building was still lighted and open, but the typewriters were silent and in Axel's office his secretary, in topcoat and head-scarf, was coming through from an inner room.

"Good timing," she smiled to Axel. "I've just put on the kettle. Will you make tea for yourself?"

"Thanks, Clara, yes. Will you stay and have some?" he asked.

"No. I had some at four, and my husband is meeting me to go to see a film in the city, so if you don't want me for anything more –?"

"Nothing has come up while I've been out?"

"No, nothing," she told him, and then left after bidding them both *goeden dag*.

The inner room, where tea-things were ready on a tray, was furnished with leather-covered chairs, bookshelves, a drinks cabinet, and a divan along the wall under a window spoke to the room's being the "pad" Axel had mentioned on Jonnet's first night. It was essentially a man's room – comfortable but austere, except for a white alabaster bowl of colourful anemones atop the bookshelves.

He stood behind her, pointing over her shoulder to the fastenings of her coat. "Better take it off, or you won't feel the benefit when you go out," he advised, and took it from her when she slipped her arms out of it and shook her hair free of her head-scarf. He invited her to a deep armchair, made the tea and brought it to her, with a plate of biscuits. Sitting opposite and stirring his own, he said, "Safe subject, one hopes – how are you getting on at the farm?"

"Better, now that I have something to do." She told him about her having taken over some of the paperwork from Grethe, adding ruefully, "I'd feel a great deal more at ease there if I got on better with Munt."

Axel laughed. "*Nobody* gets on with Munt – except Grethe herself. Why, what particular sword have you crossed with him?"

"None of my crossing. He went straight into the attack minutes after we first met."

"In front of Grethe?"

"No, we were alone. He was potting up things in the green house, and he accused me of being 'another of them' – 'another' besides Dirk, I realised – and seemed to think we both had hopes of inheriting Tante Grethe's property."

"Like that, *hm*?" Axel commented. "Well, you must admit that you both did appear on the scene rather hotfoot, just about when Grethe – if she ever will – might be considering retiring."

"And supposing she were, do you think Munt has been hoping she would leave the farm to him?"

"I should doubt it. He already has most of the power he wants, without any of the responsibility. But he could be afraid of being swept into his own retirement by the broom of a new owner. The Boerdery Handel is the only way of life he knows; *is* his life, in fact."

"Well, he needn't take out his fears on me. I've no ambitions with regard to the farm, and nor, I'm sure, has Dirk. And so I told Munt."

"Though without convincing him? However, here's a peacemaking suggestion for what it's worth. Ask him about his sport."

"His sport?"

"The freak daffodil that he calls his *Gouden Knoope* – Boss of Gold. Now and then true-coming flowers throw such sports, and some seasons back he spotted one with a deep gold rosette as its centre, in a field of orthodox coronaed blooms, and he's been cultivating it ever since."

"A kind of Black Tulip?" Jonnet suggested.

Axel's brows lifted. "So at least you've read your Dumas! But no, not exactly like. A complete new type must be grown from seed, and a record of its crossings and re-crossings kept in detail. A sport like Munt's has bypassed all this, and Munt grows his from the bulb, hoping, season after season, that it won't revert."

"And it hasn't yet?"

"No. So if you could show an intelligent interest in it, you might manage to placate him."

"Thanks. I'll try that. And if it doesn't revert, will it have a lot of commercial value?"

"Possibly, though for Munt it is Art for Art's sake, I think." He went on conversationally, "Talking of ambitions, what *are* yours in life? A career? Marriage? You have some?"

"Not like that – ambitions in the abstract. I like my work and I hope to take my Library Diploma when I'm eligible. I haven't any particular theories on marriage."

"No ideal man? No girlish dreams? Just a level-headed conviction that you can take it or leave it when the time comes?"

"I've told you, I haven't any preconceived ideas about it," Jonnet said. "Nor about the – quite nebulous man I may choose."

"Nor of the one who may choose you?"

"He might not be the same man," she pointed out.

"No indeed. But supposing he were, and you were both

64

free, doesn't your imagination conjure any pictures of the outcome?"

"Outcome – such as?" she parried.

"Surely the natural one of your both seeing marriage as the only choice open to you – about as inevitable as to-morrow's sunrise, no less?"

"Without my having even met him yet?" She shook her head. "I'm afraid my imagination isn't as vivid as all that."

"And you haven't met him yet?"

"Not recognisably –" She broke off as she saw his glance go past her to the door. He rose as it opened and Saskia Moet came in. "I did knock, but evidently you were too absorbed to hear," she said, sending an arch glance between him and Jonnet. She first refused the chair which Axel offered her, then took it and sat on its edge. "I'm not staying, so don't let me interrupt anything," she said, then addressed Axel directly.

"I called on the Herengracht, thinking you might be at home. I did find Dirk, who said you might be here, although the office would be closed, so as I had nothing better to do, I drove out."

Axel said drily, "I'm flattered. What did you want me for?"

"You and Dirk too. For a party. Oh, and of course Jonnet, but Dirk had said he would pass on the invitation to her. Naturally I didn't expect to find her tête-à-tête with you. I thought – Well anyway, Letti wants to meet her, so we're having a buffet supper on Sunday, and afterwards we'll do something – I don't know what yet. But say you can come?"

"Sunday?" he mused. "Yes, I think so." He turned to Jonnet. "What about you?"

Suppressing an idiotic impulse to pretend that she must consult a whole diaryful of engagements – Saskia had that effect on her! – Jonnet said of her entirely empty Sunday, "Yes, I'm free too. What time will you expect me?"

"You can come with me. I'll drive over for you." That was Axel's voice clashing with Saskia's "Around six, perhaps?" to which she added quickly, "You needn't do that, Axel. Dirk said he would come out for Jonnet and bring her himself." She stood then, refastened the strap of the fur-lined hood which framed her piquant little face and asked Jonnet, "How are you getting back to the farm? Can I give you a lift? That is, if you're not spending the whole evening with Axel?"

"Thanks, but I'm cycling, and I'm going now." Jonnet reached for her coat and tied her head-scarf. Axel said, "I'll see you back," and the three of them went out of the building together.

On the broad outer step Saskia paused and lifted her delicate nostrils to the sharp air. "A lovely night! Not a breath of wind, and the *stars* –! What a pity that bicycles are sheer death to romance, isn't it?" she murmured to no one in particular, then blew a kiss in Axel's direction and went over to her car.

CHAPTER FOUR

THAT night's frost was the forerunner of more. At dawn the bitter wind rose again, bringing a powdering of snow, and by full light there was treacherous black ice underfoot and the still water of rain-butts was frozen solid.

It held and grew more intense, the barometer rising by a degree or two by day, but dropping inexorably at night. Only the main roads were safe for traffic and the soil of the farm fields was ironclad. The couple of Grethe's workers who lived nearest turned up and did jobs under cover; the rest were absentee, fearing for their limbs and their bicycles on the skating-rink of the roads. The lack of busyness gave the consequent silence a quality to which it was almost possible to listen, as to a noise. Even the thrush who earlier had begun to try out his winter song was daunted now. The search for food, shelter and unfrozen water was the prime preoccupation of every wild thing.

Grethe, viewing the prospect on the fourth day of the frost, observed, "If this goes on, they will be skating on Axel Keyser's mere. You saw it, I suppose?"

"Yes." Warned of her aunt's attitude, Jonnet added non-committally, "It seems quite an ambitious scheme."

Grethe sniffed. "Ambitious? It is a madness. A bulb farm should be a bulb farm, not a funfair!"

At that Jonnet felt impelled to go to Axel's defence, however mildly. She said, "Oh, I thought it was just to be gardens and swimming and flower-beds and lawns?"

"And how short a step from there to sideshows and teas, shooting-galleries and wild parties and drinking at night?" Grethe demanded. "No, that one has too much money for a bachelor. He should marry and settle down. A wife, and a family to bring up would put an end to all that nonsense. Then he might learn the true value of hectare upon hectare of wasted land. And goodness knows he has enough girls about him, eager and willing. You'd think he could find one of good Dutch family and manners, and looks enough to match!"

(He mows the girls down, Saskia had said of Axel.) Her interest aroused for the second time by this picture of him pursued and escaping. Jonnet asked, "Hasn't his name been linked with any of them then?"

"*Maar natuurlijk!*" Grethe spread her hands. "He is a man of thirty, isn't he? And no monk. Yes, there has been this one and that one, from time to time. Just now, I do not know. I have heard nothing, and Letti, who has little more to do with her time than to gather and pass on gossip, would have been on the telephone before now if anyone new had caught his fancy."

At least the severity of the frost had gratified someone – Munt. Proved right in his insistence that the litter-cover be kept on the fields until early February, he turned comparatively genial, even sparing Grethe, who had been wrong, the "I told you so" which she claimed she deserved.

Encouraged by his change of mood, Jonnet ventured to offer her own olive branch by enquiring for his precious freak, as Axel had advised. But she was to fail.

She had gone to the greenhouse to choose a pot plant for the house and used Axel's name as an opening for her question. "Mijnheer Keyser says you are cultivating a rather rare daffodil, and might tell me about it if I asked," she said.

Munt looked up from what he was doing to glare at her. "And what business is it of yours?" he demanded.

She recoiled a little. "None, I suppose, but –"

68

"Then why try to make it so? In order, no doubt, to try to take it from me when you take all the rest? You wouldn't want it. You wouldn't know what to do with it. But it would be enough for you to have stolen it from me!"

At which point, realising that no reassurance was likely to satisfy him, she gave up. So much, she thought, for oil on troubled waters, buried hatchets or whatever, reminding herself to tell Axel of what little worth his well-meant advice had been. Munt had decided to distrust her, and that was that.

When, on Sunday, the road conditions were as bad as ever, she rang Dirk, telling him to send a taxi to take her to Saskia's party instead of his fetching her himself. He demurred, but she insisted, and as usual in argument with her, he gave in, saying that in that case he wouldn't take his own car out, but would walk or tram the short distance across the city to Tante Letti's house on the outskirts.

Saskia had not let her know what was planned for the evening, so, judging that it was likely to be a home-staying affair, she wore a long evening skirt and a batwing-sleeved jumper in silver lurex, and tied a kerchief lightly over her hair to control it for the few steps necessary to and from the taxi.

Letti Moet's house was ultra-modern, one of four facing inward to a private square, set out as gardens with a centre-piece of a fountain and surrounding ornamental basins. When Jonnet gave the taximan the address, he knew it. "Millionaire's Village, they call that quarter," he said familiarly, and treated her, throughout most of the journey, to, as it were, a taxi's-eye-view of the city's layout by class, mentioning in passing that the Herengraacht and its purlieus was where the "real" aristocrats lived.

Most of Saskia's guests, and Dirk too, were already there when Jonnet arrived. She was shown by a maid to a bedroom doing duty as a cloakroom, which was so cluttered by warm outer clothes, fur-lined boots and balaclava-type bonnets that, despite the cars, nose to bumper round the square, she concluded that a good many people had copied Dirk by giving the weather best and walking to the party.

Downstairs again, she was greeted, enfolded and kissed on both cheeks by someone as unlike Grethe as was possible, but who could only be her sister.

Tante Letti, Grethe's junior by ten years as Jonnet knew, looked far younger still. She had an elegant figure, well corseted to slimness, her beautifully arranged hair was a silvery blonde, her complexion almost unlined and her naturally light blue eyes accentuated to darkness by heavy make-up. Her voice, as she held Jonnet off from her and crooned, "Jonnet, my *dear* child! Brother Pieter's daughter! Do you know, I have been longing to meet you ever since Saskia told me you had come over to join Dirk? So good of you to endure that *arctic* farm for poor Grethe's sake –" in a voice that was lazy and die-away, reminding Jonnet that Dirk had described Letti as "limp", though to Jonnet's feminine eyes, she seemed extremely well poised and aware.

She tucked an arm into Jonnet's and began, "Now you must meet everyone else –" but then held her off again, glancing doubtfully at the full length of her dress.

"You look quite charming, but you have brought something else with you, haven't you, dear? Something rather more suitable? For skating, I mean –?" she murmured, her voice trailing away on a faint note of surprised question.

Jonnet stared, then looked about her at the crowded room. To her dismay no one else at all was in ankle-length skirts. There were jeans and there were bell-bottoms, and such skirts as there were were dirndl, pleated, mini and calf-length. But they were all of tweed or heavy jersey or wool;

70

even a couple of scarlet ones of flannel! She echoed blankly, "For *skating*? No, I haven't brought anything else. I wasn't told –"

Tante Letti shook her head. "You mean Saskia, naughty girl, didn't tell you?"

"That it was to be a skating party? No."

"Nor Dirk either? I know *he* has come prepared. For going out to Axel Keyser's place after supper. Skating by lamplight, you know. Just you young people, of course, not me."

Jonnet said, "I haven't seen Dirk, only spoken to him on the phone. But it doesn't really matter, as I don't skate."

"Oh. Well, that's different. But he should still have warned you." Letti looked about her. "Ah, there he is now, with Axel and Saskia." She beckoned to him, and the three of them came over.

Saskia said perfunctorily to Jonnet, "Sorry. I didn't see you come in. How are you?" while her stepmother addressed Axel, "What do you think? This careless little *katje,* as you call her, didn't tell Jonnet that you would be skating, so she hasn't come prepared with a thing to wear. Saskia *lieveling,* why didn't you tell her?"

Saskia pushed her lips forward in a little pout. "I suppose I forgot," she said. "When I invited her on Monday, I didn't know we were going to be able to skate. It had only just started to freeze."

"But you rang everyone else this morning and told *them.* After, of course, you –" Letti smiled archly at Axel – "had invited everyone over, as your mere would bear."

"Well, I thought Dirk would tell her," Saskia excused herself afresh.

"And I thought you would have told her," put in Dirk.

Between them they were making Jonnet feel like a badly wrapped parcel being passed from hand to hand. Nothing

71

was more galling to her sex, as both Letti and Saskia should know, than to be over-dressed or under-dressed for any function, and somehow it mattered the more to have Axel Keyser witnessing her shame. Desperate and embarrassed, she said, as she had done to Letti, "It doesn't matter in the slightest. I don't skate, and as I came by taxi, I can call another to take me home, when the rest of you leave."

But she wasn't to be allowed to retire with dignity. Their protests came in chorus, arousing the curiosity of groups of youngsters near by. And across everyone else's voice came Axel's, incisive and hectoring,

"Nonsense. If you don't try to skate when you have the chance here, you'll never learn. You'll come along." He turned to Saskia. "*Katje* my pet, you must be able to fix Jonnet up with something. Boots, skates, whatever you would wear yourself – something warm for her head?"

Saskia, more kittenlike than ever in the briefest of circular black skirts and black polo-necked sweater, looked Jonnet up and down and allowed reluctantly, "Skates, yes. There are several spare pairs knocking about. Boots too, perhaps." Her glance had appraised the slim ankles and feet of which Jonnet was justly proud. "But she is a lot bigger than I am. I haven't a thing that would fit her."

"Oh, Saskia darling," Letti urged again, "perhaps nothing of yours *now*. You have fined down so, these last few months, haven't you? To think –" she invited Axel and Dirk to think with her – "that we used to be able to tease you about your puppy-fat! Or should it have been kitten-fat?" she appealed to Axel, before continuing directly to Saskia, "What about one of your old school skirts, when you were something rather shameful round your waist? You could look out for Jonnet one of those, surely?"

Saskia said, "Oh, *those*!" – a disparagement of skirts which were of shaming measurements round the waist, with which Jonnet heartily though silently agreed, as Saskia linked Dirk by the arm and offered a hand to Axel, saying, "Well, that's all about that, thank goodness. We can dress-rehearse after supper. So let's get these layabouts dancing or something. They can't be expecting their supper *yet*."

At that, murmuring a word about "seeing to other people", Letti drifted away too, leaving Jonnet standing alone until she saw that Axel seemed to be waiting for her, allowing the other two to go on.

She joined him, her mood ready for battle. Almost beween her teeth she muttered, "You needn't have been a party to that. You know I couldn't skate, so there wasn't any point to it, and you could have let me back out gracefully. I wanted to."

"Leaving poor little *katje* and Dirk in the wrong? Shame on you! Besides, I wasn't a mere party to it. I organised it, if you noticed?" he claimed loftily.

"I did," she said. "Making a – a charity jumble sale of me! I must say that the next time I achieve a social *gaffe* of this size, I hope you won't be there, weighing in with help."

"Don't worry, I shan't be," he soothed.

"Good!"

"– If only because you wouldn't have been guilty of this one, if you'd been warned. You would have been here in your own merry skating gear, hired skates and boots – the lot. *Showing* us, in fact."

"I should not. I can't skate – need I say it again? – and I should have made an excuse to stay away."

"Which would have been a mistake and unfair to your education, for which I've made myself responsible. You're going to put a good face on wearing Saskia's cast-offs and get up on those blades and skate, even if you progress half on them, and half on your overturned ankles. In the meantime, try to *look* as if I were your dearest buddy, and come along. I suppose at least you can dance?"

She could and did – with him until he passed her on to a shy youth of whom, though he asked her to have supper with him, she learned little but that his name was Franck and that he was a naval cadet on leave, who knew few more people at the party than she did herself.

Supper was a self-service affair. Jonnet saw Dirk at a table for two with Saskia, with whom he had stayed continually so far. Axel was one of a party of six. Tante Letti played attentive hostess from table to table in turn, refusing to settle anywhere, saying that her beauty diet allowed her only a cup of clear soup and a fragment of minute steak in the evening, neither of which was on the hearty menu her cook had provided for her guests.

After supper, when a concerted move was made to get ready for the trip in shared cars, Jonnet parted from Franck when Saskia came for her, taking her to her own room to be equipped. Laced skating boots and skates proved no problem – there was a cupboardful of them, and after some trial and error Jonnet was provided with an elastic-waisted navy serge skirt, a thick white cardigan and a bala-clava, with woollen gauntlet mitts and knee-length oversocks for her legs. Of her discarded evening things Saskia advised carelessly, "You can leave them here and Dirk can collect them for you," which confirmed for Jonnet that Dirk was a fairly frequent visitor to "Millionare's Village."

Axel's lake, which on Monday had been troubled grey water, was tonight a still white floor under the stars, lighted from its surrounding shingle by lamps of closed carriage-lantern type. And when the cars had discharged their loads, someone had the bright idea of facing them to the water, so that their headlights illuminated it too.

Laughing and chatting, people darted in and out of the

shadows, looking for somewhere to sit while they strapped on their skates. Jonnet, using a pile of timber for a seat, pretended to have difficulty with hers, in order to let the boy and two girls with whom she had travelled get on to the ice before her. She hadn't confessed that she couldn't skate, so on her assurance that she would soon follow them, they tip-tapped away, leaving her alone. Once on the ice, the boy and one of the girls paired off and glided away together; the other girl, after experimenting with a few pirouettes and glissés was claimed by another man, and Jonnet, with no one near her for the moment, finished her strapping and ventured to stand on her blades.

Sure enough, she could stand — as long as she kept a handhold on the timber. But letting go of it and taking a first tentative step down the shingle, both ankles wobbled and collapsed outward, and as her arms flailed wildly for balance, her hands were caught from behind, her arms brought forcibly down to her sides, and there was a taut masculine body close at her back.

It was Axel's, of course. It *would* be, she thought, mortified. He had his skates slung over his arm and he had approached her across grass. He looked up at her as he sat down to put on his skates. "You should have waited for me," he said. "Even I didn't expect you to go solo straight away."

"I thought at least I could stand on the things," she said crossly. "Other people can walk on theirs."

"Ah, but they've altered your centre of gravity, and your body has to adapt to a new one." He stood up and went close behind her again. "Now, we're going to play ponies; my hands on each side of your waist — *so*, and we walk down to the ice at your pace, not mine."

They set out. When her ankles wobbled, his hold tightened, steadying her, and when they reached the ice and she was actually standing upright, he changed his grip to stand at her side, cross-handed with her in the orthodox partnering position. "Now for that centre of gravity – lean forward, bend your knees and keep them bent. So – straight ahead on your outside foot ... good. This inside one next. There! We've moved. Now again. No, *forward*, girl. You're not attempting the splits!" – as her foot went out at a perilous tangent – "Yes, that's better. Take it easy. Away we go –"

Head lowered, lip bitten in fierce concentration, clutching his hands in a drowning man's grip, only too aware that people were watching, only too determined not to appear more of a raw tyro than she need, she tried. Now it was easier – a little. Now, forward by at least a dozen glides without mishap. Now in a bad patch, first one ankle wringing over, then the other; right foot too close to left and tripping her, skates tangling. Axel appearing patient, even if he didn't feel it. Now again easy, and for further than before. Smooth gliding, even rhythmic. She could throw her head back now, taking the bite of the air on her glowing cheeks. This was wonderful! Travel in a new orbit! She didn't want to stop when Axel halted and ruled, "That's fine – in harness. But now alone."

She clung to his hands. "I can't –"

But he was already behind her, his hands again on her hips at first, then taking them away. She tottered slightly, forgot to lean forward, then remembered; kept her balance over her bent knees, dared her ankles to give way, and went forward – alone.

She hadn't learned how to stop by herself, and when she did her feet betrayed her by sliding apart alarmingly. But Axel was there, and so was his arm, going round her and holding her until she steadied and looked up at him, her eyes probably as alight with triumph as she felt.

"I can! I did, didn't I? Well, a little," she claimed.

He laughed. "For once, modesty becomes you. But yes, given a bit more time and practice, you could be a natural, I'd say."

"Are we likely to get more time? Will the frost hold?" she asked eagerly.

"Doubtful, now we're into February, and though it could, it would be a mixed blessing for us bulb folk. We don't want it as late as this in the winter." Axel broke off to signal to Dirk, who was passing at speed with Saskia. "*He*, you!" he called. "Come and take a turn with your sister."

"Next time round," Dirk called back. As they went on Jonnet followed them with her eyes, wishing that reluctance to discuss Dirk forbade her commenting that he had spent the whole evening with Saskia, and getting Axel's reaction. But as if he read her thoughts, Axel himself said, "You are not too sympathetic to that affair, I gather?"

She brought her glance back to him. "I don't know that it is an affair. Do you?" she countered.

"By all the signs – It was burgeoning before you arrived. But you don't approve?"

"What makes you think I don't?"

"For one thing, because you won't admit you're transparent enough to let it show. For another, you and Saskia don't jell and never could. She's a feminine type to her fingertips – all kitten charm and the kind of man-awareness that makes a chap feel good. Whereas you –"

"You're saying that, in comparison with Saskia, I'm not feminine at all?"

"Let's say that in open competition with her brand of attraction for men, you'd find yourself well down the field."

Jonnet's chin went up. "Then isn't it fortunate for me that she and I aren't in competition on any count?"

77

Axel's nod agreed. "On her experienced terms, very. But besides all that —"

"Yes?" she invited as he paused.

But he shook his head. "Nothing. Forget it. I haven't enough evidence to judge, I realise."

"Which to date hasn't always deterred you from doing it, has it?" she retorted, but was cheated of whatever riposte he might have made by the arrival of Dirk and Saskia, coming to a graceful circling halt beside them.

Saskia immediately claimed Axel when he passed Jonnet over to Dirk. But in the pause Jonnet had lost confidence, and Dirk was not as efficient a guide as Axel. Wanting to impress him, she tried too hard; the magic had gone out of the new experience, and she wasn't sorry when Dirk suggested they join the mass troop back to the shingle for the coffee and hot soup which was being dispensed from thermos flasks.

While they had been skating she had been puzzled and irked by Dirk's proficiency, and now she asked him, "How did you learn to ice-skate? In England you hadn't any more of a clue than I have now."

"I know," he said. "But it's so taken for granted here that one can skate that I decided I must learn."

"How did you? I thought this was supposed to be the only bearing frost they have had this winter?"

"So it is. But there are indoor rinks in Amsterdam, and I went to one of them nearly every week during last school term."

"You never mentioned it. You took lessons there? By yourself?"

"At first. Later, when I wasn't still making a fool of myself, Saskia often came with me. I didn't want her to, while I spent more time spreadeagled on the ice than I did on my feet."

78

"Why not? She's only a sort of – of secondhand cousin," Jonnet disparaged.

"She's not even that. She's no relation to us at all. Anyway, what about taking some lessons? If you want to, I can give you the address of this rink," Dirk offered.

"All right. Not that there's much point in it – for me," Jonnet agreed indifferently, privately resolved to make no spectacle of herself at any rink frequented by Saskia Moet. But Dirk had said that in the city there was choice, and he had put an idea into her mind.

There was some more skating after that, and Jonnet's supper partner, Franck, found her, reproaching her for failing to tell him she couldn't skate and offering to partner her now. She went round the mere with him once, but it was none too successful a trip. Neither Dirk nor he expected as much of her as Axel had done, and in consequence she couldn't give it. So, thanking him, she sent him to find another partner, telling him she was tired, had had enough, was going to take off her skates, and would watch from the shingle.

She did, for a time. Then other people's enthusiasm waned; they drifted off the ice in ones and twos until it was empty of all but one couple – Axel and Saskia, giving a near-professional exhibition turn to the rhythmic clapping of their onlookers. Standing near Jonnet, Dirk muttered morosely, "Darned nice of her to bother with me at all, when she can skate like that," for which piece of gratuitous humility, Jonnet wanted to slap him.

Now the party was breaking up. Engines were being revved, cars turned, and people were piling into them. Presumably everyone meant to go back to the Moet's house, but for Jonnet, within less than a kilometre of the farm, this seemed foolish, and she said so to Dirk, who agreed. "Saskia drove me and two other people, so I'll ask her to cram you in as well and drive round by Tante Grethe's to drop you," he said.

Consulted, Saskia said none too graciously, "I suppose I can," and Dirk took the front seat beside her. Her passengers in the back made room for Jonnet and she was about to join them when Axel drove past and stopped. "What goes?" he asked.

Dirk leaned out to explain, and Axel opened the passenger door of his own car. "No need for you to make a detour," he told Saskia across Dirk. "The fellow I brought over seems to have ditched me, so I've an empty car and can see Jonnet home."

At once Saskia was ready to make Jonnet welcome. "Oh no, we can take her," she murmured. "She won't crowd us at all."

"All the same, she will crowd me less," Axel insisted, adding to Jonnet a crisp "Come!" which, after thanking Saskia for the party, she obeyed, feeling once more like an encumbrance which people would be glad to have been spared.

On the way Axel asked, "Why didn't Dirk come over for you by car, so that he could have driven you back?"

"Because I told him not to. In view of the road conditions, I mean."

"He has had to drive in them all the week. He would have been safe enough. But does one gather that he always does what you tell him?"

She considered the question. "Mostly, I think," she said.

"Why does he?"

"I suppose because I'm often right, and he sees reason at the end of most arguments that we have."

Axel threw her an ironic glance. "What a self-satisfied little madam you are!" he commented. "But it's much as I thought. Dirk may propose, but you *dis*pose, out of some fount of superior judgement. Tell me, though, how do you come to terms whenever he may choose to defy you? As, for instance, he probably did when he went to lodge with Grethe at the farm?"

Jonnet stared ahead into the darkness. "When he was coming to Holland to teach, that was my idea, not his," she said.

"Yours?"

"Mine. When he was coming over, I had to persuade him that he ought to get in touch with such of the family as were here. You sound surprised at that?" She had meant that he should be.

He nodded. "I am," he agreed. "However, it was right for Dirk, but not right for you? Why not?"

"As he was coming, I thought that was enough, and I had other plans."

"So you send him with an open mind, and you come with yours closed like a clam. However, it all bears out a theory for which I told you earlier tonight I thought I hadn't enough evidence. Now I have."

"Indeed? And what theory is that?" she enquired loftily.

"That, as you've always had Dirk as a kind of Yes-man to decisions which you could well leave to him, you resent his appearing to say No to you over Saskia, fully as much as you resent Saskia herself. Could I be right perhaps?"

Jonnet exhaled a long indignant breath. "I don't 'resent' Saskia," she denied. "What an idea!"

"No? Now I thought your inferiority complex in the matter of the right clothes and her skating prowess stood out a mile tonight," he countered.

"Well, the whole thing had put me in a false position through no fault of my own," she defended herself. And then, fearing that he might hear that as a lame surrender, she suddenly flared.

81

He had halted the car at the entrance to the farm, and she turned in her seat to face him.

"All right," she said. "I *don't* care for Saskia and I *do* doubt that she is the right girl for Dirk. What's more, I'd hope I'd be able to make him see it. But if it arises, it's my problem, not yours, and I'll thank you not to – to preen yourself over having guessed how I feel, how I tick. Because you have only guessed – you can't *know*. You don't, I assure you, know me at all. And come to that" – she was choking on the words now – "I can't think, having got me taped and graphed and docketed as you claim, why you bother with me any further. Unless, of course, baiting me does something splendidly warming to your ego. And if that isn't the reason, then it certainly isn't out of any concern for me. *That* I know for sure!"

There she stopped, both for want of the breath she had used so rashly and because, just very slightly, she was aghast at her own outburst. But he had driven her to it. It had had to be said. Not looking at him, she waited for his reaction, and when it came it was two words, spoken very softly, "So there!"

She glanced up at him. "What do you mean – 'So there'?"

"You forgot to add it. Isn't it the accepted English exit line for a bit of nursery head-tossing like yours? 'Yackety-yackety-yack, boum, boum – and so *there*!' Isn't that they way it should have gone?"

"You can forget the nursery crack. I'm not a child, just stamping her foot in temper," she muttered.

"Nor yet a woman in some ways. You're top-heavy with juvenile candour and pretty lightweight on adult finesse. For instance, can you hear Saskia asking a man pointblank why he bothers with her, as you did just now? Not she – in so many words. Her feminine radar would tell her that if he has given a second thought to a girl after his first, something about her must have intrigued him enough to make the set-up interesting – possibly to them both. And for the time being she would settle for that."

Jonnet said tautly, "I see. A useful short cut, this radar – if one has it. But will you please stop quoting Saskia Moet at me? You've admitted yourself that she and I are poles apart, and when I want to learn something, I'm afraid I have to ask."

"In this case, why, following the first unfortunate impression you let me gain of you, I listened to my second thoughts?"

"I suppose so –"

"Well, how about this? At first I wasn't to know I could have the chance to play Petruchio, taming a sharp-tongued, ill-informed Katharina, but once I had taken it on, I found I quite enjoyed the role – and still do. So does that satisfy you as to the how and the why of my second thoughts?"

Inwardly flinching at "sharp-tongued" and "ill-informed", Jonnet said, "Adequately, thank you. Especially as it isn't the first time you've said you relish having me as a target. And though you can hardly expect me to appreciate being seen as a shrew or – or an Aunt Sally, don't let me spoil your fun, will you?"

He laughed aloud at that. "I won't," he promised. "Though I still suspect you share it with me on occasion – as now."

"Now?"

"Yes." He looked at the luminous hands of his watch. "As evidence, we've been stationary here for upward of five minutes. You could have been cosily in the house and I on my way by now. So can you honestly claim, hand on heart, that you didn't prefer to pick a stimulating quarrel with me?"

She gasped. "Of course I can! I don't deliberately pick quarrels. I didn't then –"

"On the contrary, you didn't launch your frontal attack until we stopped. And if you haven't enjoyed the clash it caused, why are you still here?"

"I'm not! That is, I'm just going," she claimed, confused. And then, suddenly struck by the utter absurdity of quarrelling with him *about* quarrelling, she bit her lip, wanting to laugh.

He was watching her quizzically. "That's better," he said. "But what's the joke?"

When she told him, he countered, "What did I tell you? The thing has the seeds of humour in it all along the way." He got out of the car with her and took and held the hand she offered him. Finding it difficult, she said in a low voice, "I still haven't thanked you for – most of tonight."

He weighed her hand lightly in his own. "Nor I you – for the unique experience of seeing that light of achievement in your eye when you found you could skate alone. At that moment you weren't even your own age. You were Universal Child, taking its first walking step and telling the world."

Not knowing what to reply to that, she hesitated. "You'd been – very kind. But it didn't last. Later I couldn't do a thing right."

"Just as well. You were saved from getting too pleased with yourself too soon," he retorted, and as she opened her mouth to protest, he released her hand and flicked the tip of her nose with his forefinger. "Coming to the boil again? Don't," he advised.

"I'm not. I wasn't. I'm going in now. Good night."

"Just a moment –" Without touching her he bent and touched her lips lightly with his own. "By way of a pipe of peace," he explained to her involuntary wince of surprise.

"When are you going to allow me to show you Amsterdam?"

"Do you want to show me Amsterdam?"

"I *have* to show you Amsterdam – as part of your set course. But we can leave it until the weather is kindlier. I'll ring you and make a date."

Though she didn't look round, she knew he waited until she went into the house. Inside, she leaned back against the closed door, putting the palms of her gloved hands to her cold cheeks, then fingers to her lips, remembering the kiss which had been so out of context with the pattern of their relationship.

As a peace-making gesture it had no more value than a pat on the head and a soothing, "There, there!" And between Axel Keyser and herself it had asked no warmth of response from her. Which made of the friendlier note on which they had parted nothing that promised any change from the cut-and-thrust which he claimed to enjoy. The next time they met some provocative word of his or some unguarded one of hers would cause the sparks to fly again between them. They acted on each other like allergies. And yet tonight she herself was aware of a change, a moving on from the hostility into which he could goad her so easily, towards a curiosity about Axel, a need to know him better. And if in his kiss she had read any such interested question to her, she could have answered it willingly, she thought.

But there hadn't been. Why should she expect it? With a smothered exclamation of distaste, she thrust away from the door and locked it as if, with her savage turn of its heavy key, she were shutting an unbidden and repellent mind-picture out.

. . . Axel, at the climax of his exhibition bout with Saskia, sweeping her high into a final "lift", then with a finely controlled movement, setting her down and planting a kiss full upon her mouth, before they parted and whirled away from each other to the limits of the ice . . .

Kissing Saskia with flair, as he had kissed her with easy confidence, thought Jonnet. *Saskia* – about whose practised coquetry she would have said he had few illusions! Kissing her in public and in full view of Dirk, whose courtship of Saskia he claimed to champion. Yet Dirk had seemed to take the kiss as part of the show. So why couldn't she? Because – because she objected to being at the receiving end of kisses which were tossed around like confetti. *That* was why! *And* why she wanted to forget the short-lived pleasure which had followed her stab of surprise at Axel's kiss for her. For that was just about as expendable as his claim that he meant it as a peace-offering. He didn't want to make peace with her. He had said as much only a few minutes earlier. He was enjoying the war.

CHAPTER FIVE

THE frost did not hold. Twenty-four hours later the long icicles from the house eaves were dripping, the roads were wet and the ice lids on the field dykes were in splinters. The air turned balmy, the sun began to have strength enough to pierce the early morning cloud, and the earth seemed to open up to the pressure of the eager growth it had been nurturing and guarding through the winter.

The farm turned busy. Munt permitted the peat cover to come off the fields, even from the low-lying frost-prone Laag Veld, and very soon then they turned from brown to green as the ranked spikes of the daffodils came through. In the small "home" field nearest to the house, there was a thrifty planting of autumn-sown onions and radish and lettuce between the bulb rows, under cloches. There was hoeing and mulching, and when the daffodil spikes had become leaves, the tulips had broken ground and were showing.

"It will be a good and early spring," the optimists said. And the pessimists, "We shall suffer for this". Munt was a pessimist; Tante Grethe was an optimist; Jonnet, who hadn't often seen spring come to the countryside, only to the city, made the most of the gentle present, hoping she had seen the worst of what a Dutch winter could do.

As the afternoons lengthened she cycled out more and further afield, exploring the easy roads and often reporting back to Grethe the state of progress of the bulbs on their neighbours' holdings – a mild form of espionage which Grethe called "keeping abreast". And it was on one such cycle ramble that, returning to the farm just as dusk was falling, Jonnet had the experience of a surge of feeling for the beauty of the landscape about her.

It was a curious sensation – almost as if she had rubbed blurred eyes and cleared them of their jaundiced vision. For the scene was by now a familiar one – the great stretch of unhedged, brown-green fields; the only trees in sight some bare pollard willows bordering a reed bed running alongside the road; the neighbouring windmill in stark silhouette against the sky, still luminous from the rays of a sun already gone down below the horizon.

She had looked at the same panorama a dozen times at about the same time of day – had looked at it, but hadn't seen it as she was seeing it now – typically Dutch, utterly alien, but not any longer the taken-for-granted last stretch of a cycle ride. It was gentle and quiet and full of character, waiting for spring, and she found herself thinking, "It has got something. It's not just tourist postcard stuff. It's alive, and if it had always been my scene, I would love it, want to defend it. *I could even defend it now*" – a switch of outlook which so astonished her that, as she rode on after dismounting to stare, she wondered how far she could afford to trust the sincerity of the thought which had followed it – "Supposing chance decreed that I should spend the rest of my life here, should I still see it as a prison sentence or not?"

Meanwhile she had booked and attended some skating lessons at a rink in the city. She hadn't told Dirk at first, but when she did, she often made a habit of calling in for a cup of tea with him after his return from afternoon school. He questioned idly why she hadn't let him recommend a rink to her, but he didn't question her change of mind about its being worth her while to learn, and she was glad of that. For it was something which she found it difficult to explain to herself. It wasn't likely, people said, that there would be any more hard frosts this winter, and by next year the whole Dutch interlude would be behind her. So it had to be that to try to learn to skate with a bit of style and grace, was merely for her own satisfaction. She wasn't going to have the chance to show off to Saskia or to Dirk or to – well, to anyone.

Because of the state of the roads until the thaw, she hadn't been able to keep her promise to visit little Lysbet Bernard again, and by now the child would be back at school. So Jonnet chose a Saturday to ride over and see her, only to find she was not at home. "My son Berik, her father, has taken her into the city to a children's film show," said Mevrouw Bernard. "But you are very welcome, Mejuffrouw Handel. Won't you come in and take *koffietafel* with me? I was just about to have mine."

Jonnet accepted, as Grethe was out, and she needn't get back for lunch at the farm. She asked after Lysbet and heard she was fully well again. Mevrouw Bernard bustled about, laying the table with cheese and rye bread and doughnuts and a bowl of fruit, and asking Jonnet's preference for coffee or beer or tea or a soft drink.

Jonnet chose tea; the old lady took coffee. They talked about the frost, the near prospect of spring, and how well the flowers were likely to time their blossoming for the Corso – the great parade of flower-decorated floats from Sassenheim through Lisse on a fifteen-kilometre route at the end of April, which, according to Mevrouw Bernard, "the whole world" attended.

"All the great farms send floats," she told Jonnet. "The Corso, you see, is arranged at the time of the de-heading of the flowers, so as they serve the purpose of decorating the floats, they are not wasted. There are judges, and prizes for the best floats. Last year, that of Het Wijdelande was a Viking ship in tulips and hyacinths and it won a third prize. This year's design is still a secret; even Berik, who works

89

for Mijnheer Keyser, does not know what it is to be."

Remembering her first morning's whimsy, Jonnet said, "I'm glad they use the flowers for something instead of just throwing them away. Who designs the floats, and who does the work on them?"

"For the Mijnheer? Ah, he goes often to England on business, and he has an English friend who is an artist in display. This man comes over to stay with the Mijnheer at the time of the Corso. They decide on the idea and the design, and all of us – yes, the estate workers and their wives and children too – help to dress the spectacle, whatever it may be. It is a busy time – the work takes several days to finish – but the Mijnheer is so good that we all do our best for him. As your neighbour, you are getting to know him well now, *mejuffrouw*?"

How to answer that? Could she claim with truth to "know" Axel at all? Jonnet said carefully, "I haven't seen very much of him. But yes, perhaps a little better than I did at first."

"When he made jokes at your expense, some of them a little cruel, I thought? He does not do this any more, I hope?"

"Sometimes he does. At other times he can choose to be very kind."

"And when he does not choose, that hurts you? It stings?"

"It might, if I let it. But now, if he criticises me for being what I am . . . as I am, I confess I flare up."

"You have a hot temper, *mejuffrouw*?"

Jonnet hesitated. "I wouldn't have said I had. Until –"

"– Until, when he is not being as kind as one knows he can be, he judges you unfairly, you think, and then you answer back?"

"That's about it, I suppose," Jonnet agreed wryly.

The old lady did not answer for a moment. Then, "And this says nothing to you?" she suggested.

"This?" Jonnet's echo was sharp. "What?"

"This readiness to quarrel with Mijnheer Keyser; this temper of yours which he arouses when he hurts you, even though you deny he can. Now to *me* that says it matters to you what he says to you, what he shows he thinks of you. And when his opinion of you is not as you would like it to be, then I think you care too much."

Jonnet denied hotly, "I care no more than I would about anyone who tried to put me in the wrong, when I may only be – well, a bit hasty or mistaken."

"Yet I think it would not annoy you, if you did not care." Mevrouw Bernard paused. "You must forgive me, my dear, but I am an old woman, and living a long time, I know that only the people with the power to hurt you can rouse you to deep anger and the need to fight back. Only when friends or lovers quarrel do they suffer and perhaps scold. Others can just differ and need not care if they lose a friend."

"But if I quarrelled with any other of my friends as I do with Mijnheer Keyser, I should expect to lose them," said Jonnet.

"Though I think, only if they wanted to be lost to you; or if you wanted to lose them. For you I believe it is different. When the Mijnheer is kind, you do not want to lose him, and whether or not *you* are kind, he may not want to lose you, however often he trails the coat –" Mevrouw Bernard broke off. "You understand me? You have perhaps the same meaning of words in English?"

Jonnet nodded. "Yes, just the same. And you're right about him. He admits he does sometimes trail his coat to provoke me; he enjoys having me as a target is how he puts it."

"As I thought. He does not want you to escape him alto-gether. And you, *mejuffrouw*, when you scold, you enjoy yourself too?"

"I did at first. Now –" Jonnet sketched a long curve on the tablecloth with her thumbnail – "now I am not sure that I do."

"Because he wins more often than you do? Or because you would now prefer it that you both could be kind to each other?"

"No. Yes. Oh, I really don't know –" As Jonnet looked up in apology for her vagueness, Mevrouw Bernard smiled, and said,

"And it is unfair to press you, if you are not sure – about him. But when, one day, you do know whether you are fighting a man for fighting's sake, or fighting to keep him near you, then you will think of me and may say to your-self, 'Perhaps she was a little wise, that old one – she knew that love does not always wear a happy face. It can still be there between two people – even when it frowns.' But come – your plate has been empty for too long. What will you take now? Some fruit? These apples are from Berik's own storing; he is able to keep them from October until March."

Jonnet chose an apple, recognising the tact with which Mevrouw Bernard had turned the subject, and was grate-ful. Of course the old lady was only talking in a general way; being sage before the event of some love affair which she must know Jonnet hadn't experienced yet. But all the same her advice had stemmed from their talk of Axel, and Jonnet was reluctant to be forced to laugh off any idea that, as far as she was concerned, love and Axel Keyser had a context at all.

And yet when she had parted from Mevrouw Bernard and was on her way home she remembered the phrase, "fighting to keep him near you", and her honesty wondered . . . wondered and accused her.

Was it so? Was she also enjoying the war – enjoying it too much to be willing for it to worsen into bitterness, to sour completely, which it hadn't yet? She looked at that thought, envisaging the far side of some deep difference which would part them irrevocably. Would she regret it if they had to avoid each other; never spoke again either as friends or as sparring partners, each of them polite, if they had to be for form's sake; otherwise enemies?

Her heart missed a beat, then quickened and thumped as she knew the answer to that was Yes and *Yes*. She didn't want to lose Axel's cool interest in her to any quarrel . . . to anything. And honesty took the truth even further. She didn't want to lose Axel – full stop. Which meant – didn't it? – that for her, though not for him, love and he were in context after all. *She was beginning to fall in love with him* – secretly wanted to hear his name spoken by Mevrouw Bernard, by Tante Grethe, by Dirk, by anyone; wanted to discover him, explore him, know him – wanted him to care to know *her*.

By the measure of their challenge to each other she had thought herself aloof from the girls who, according to Saskia, were mown down by his charm. But now she was jealous of them, curious about them. Was there one in particular for him? Or was he – the slang for it was "playing the field"? And when he had kissed her and she hadn't resisted him, in his eyes did that make her one of "the field"? Or supposing – just supposing – she had made her response warmer, might he have kissed her again – and differently? . . . On and on and round and round went the questions, even those without any answers a trap from which she didn't want to escape. In order not to break the spell of loving Axel and knowing it, she rode on past the farm and far out across the country which had begun to charm her un-

93

beknownst to her will. As Axel had done – by looks, voice, mastery, kindness, by his very unawareness of his hold upon her, by being simply himself. Now even the very landscapes which she shared with him spoke of him and his love for them. Another question – that afternoon when she had *seen* them, as it were for the first time – had she loved them because of him, and hadn't known it?

She remembered with pleasure that they had parted for once in peace and on a promise from him. He hadn't fulfilled it yet. But he would. And when they met, though he wouldn't know it, there would be something new and warmly exciting between them. They wouldn't quarrel ...

When at last she returned to the farm it was dusk and Grethe was waiting supper for her. Jonnet apologised – she had cycled further than she meant to, hadn't realised the time, but wouldn't be more than a minute or two about washing her hands. And knew, when Grethe nodded approval of the glow in her cheeks, claiming, "You are taking benefit from our good Dutch air. You haven't any longer the pasty look you had when you arrived," that the glow had far less to do with air, Dutch or whatever, than with inward, secret excitement.

It didn't last, of course, if only because love, content at first with the little of a remembered exchange, a treasured look, a fraternal kiss, too soon turned greedy and wanted more. It doubted more too – sometimes even doubting that itself was mere infatuation which had no future in a sane world. Whenever the telephone rang she caught her breath, expectant. But it was always Dirk or a business call for Grethe. Axel did not ring.

Every morning she was busy with her aunt's clerical affairs and was learning to understand and talk in bulb-trade terms. On two afternoons a week she cycled into Amsterdam for her skating lessons, which she enjoyed to the full as she gained confidence at each one.

It was after one such session that she went as usual to Dirk's apartment. Sometimes he wasn't back from school when she arrived, but she had a key and would let herself in and have tea ready for him when he did come. Today, however, his door was unlocked, which didn't surprise her, as she knew it was a half-holiday for him.

She went straight in, pausing at a sound which wasn't talk, but a kind of crooning chuckle from the far side of the closed door to his sitting-room. She waited for a moment, then opened the door, only to halt on the threshold, unnoticed by the two wholly absorbed people within.

Dirk and – Saskia. Both half sitting on the edge of a settee, turned to each other, she in his arms, her graceful head thrown back as he kissed her throat while she made little crooning sounds of pleasure and laughter, before he cupped her face between his hands and kissed her long and deep upon her lips.

Jonnet, watching, bit her lip, catching back her "Hi!" of greeting to Dirk. They hadn't seen her ... didn't know – The door obeyed her silent closing of it, then blindly she turned to run – out from the outer door, across the cobbled pavement – and straight, face to face, body to body, with Axel. He broke their collision by holding her off with both hands on her forearms. He noticed first her skates which were slung from her elbow, and grinned down at her.

"Found yourself some private ice?" he quipped. "Now you could have fooled me – I thought it was spring!"

She had heard from Dirk that he had gone again to England, and didn't know he was back. Before seeing him again she had expected the small grace of a telephone call; he would suggest a date for showing her Amsterdam; she would keep it, inwardly excited, prepared to meet his mood whatever it might be; she might have rehearsed some of the things she would say to him; she would have had time to plan to look her best for him. But now this headlong encounter had cheated her. She followed his glance at her skates and stammered, "I – I've been having a skating lesson at the Meyer Rink. I've just been to see Dirk, but he –"

– "Wasn't at home? Wasn't glad to see you? Was taking a bath? Was doing a bit of counterfeiting? Setting up an illicit still? You look, if I may say so, as if you had encountered your Bad Fairy on your way out!"

She couldn't summon a smile. "Yes, he was in, but –" She stopped again.

"But obviously was up to something of which you don't approve," Axel prompted. "Well, suppose that for once you respect his right to a little private crime now and again, and come in with me instead? I'll give you some tea, if that is what you came for. You look as if you need it."

As he spoke he turned her about, a firm hand at her back. She shrugged it off. "No. I'm going home. My bike –"

He looked back at it, propped against the kerb, then left her in order to sling it into the back of his estate car nearby, and returned. "I shall be going out there myself later and I'll drive you," he said. "You may go when I'm ready, not before. Now –"

Jonnet protested weakly, "Dirk will hear us," but he took no notice. He put her in the salon, surrounded by the Delft ware and the silver-cabinets, and went through himself to the dining-room and the kitchen from where, through the open doors, she heard the turning of taps and the chink of tea things. He came back with a tray, poured tea briskly, handed her a cup and said "Now –?" again, expectantly.

Jonnet stirred her tea, keeping her head lowered. At last she said, "It was Dirk. There, next door – with Saskia."

"And so?" Axel invited unhelpfully.

96

"I opened the door on them. They didn't see me. They were kissing. And – and not just flirting. In a intimate way. You could tell it wasn't the first time. Dirk was – was being urgent, sort of involved."

"He'd be more to blame if he were kissing her *without* being involved," was Axel's dry comment on that. "Anyway, what of it? Why all the shock? I already told you that was the way things were going for Dirk, and I thought you agreed."

"Not willingly. I didn't want to believe it."

"Why not? Just because you despise Saskia as a light-weight, and are jealous of her too?"

"I am *not* jealous of Saskia. It's simply that I know she is not the right girl for Dirk." None of this was going as it should. This first meeting with Axel should have been a thing of secret delight. As it was, they weren't even quarrelling on level terms; he was sitting in judgement on her concern for Dirk, making it sound like prejudice. She heard him laugh incredulously, as if he doubted his hearing of her last remark.

"And who are you, to choose between one girl and another for Dirk? Couldn't you leave him to do that?" he enquired. "But having decided against Saskia for him, what do you propose to do about it, may I ask?"

Jonnet set aside her cup, feeling that to drink his tea in these circumstances would choke her. She said, "I shall have to tell Dirk that I saw them, and I shall ask him how far it has gone. And when he tells me, I shall talk to him and hope that I can make him see reason."

"Giving as *your* reasons merely the pricking of your thumbs of bias against Saskia?"

"Not at all. If he weren't suddenly blind, he could sum her up for himself. For one thing, she is so aware of her success with men that she would never allow him any peace about them. Already she teases him that she can get any one she wants. I've heard her. She even once" – Jonnet hesitated over this last throw to convince Axel, then made it – "boasted to him and to me that she might make a bid for *you* and would succeed."

Axel's blue eyes glinted. "Did she indeed? Well, at that I mightn't make it too difficult for her. She has her attractions – But you propose to list her faults, as you see them, to Dirk, and really expect him to be grateful to you for showing him the light?"

"Not grateful, I daresay. He won't want to listen if he is serious about Saskia. But that won't stop me. Someone must stand up for him after all."

"You don't stand up for him. You stand *on* him," Axel retorted. "You've admitted as much, and on your own showing he usually gives in to you. But this time is different. This time you aren't going to give him a curtain lecture on Saskia's shortcomings. That is, you won't if you are wise, which I begin to doubt."

Jonnet said tautly, "Thank you. You are frank. Though why shouldn't I, if I can see that she would make him unhappy, and he can't? Anyway, who is going to stop me?"

It was a defiant invitation to him to retort, "*I* am." But instead he said almost mildly, "No one can, if you are really set on a direct approach which can't help but fail with any man of spirit. If such a situation needs handling at all, it calls for a lot more finesse than that. Criticise Saskia to Dirk's face, and you are going to antagonise him against *you*, not against her. And do you really want that?"

"It needn't happen."

Axel shrugged. "All right. Risk it, if you must." He glanced at her rejected cup. "More tea?"

"No, thank you." She drew the cup towards her and gulped down the tepid liquid. He stood up. "Then perhaps we'll be on our way. I gather you don't want to intrude on the scene next door again?"

Obediently she went with him. Nothing more was said on the subject until they reached the farm. Then, hoping it sounded like a decision she might or might not take, Jonnet asked, "So supposing I don't tell Dirk that I know about him and Saskia, what then?"

"You wait until he confides in you, then play it by ear – carefully. If he doesn't tell you himself, you still wait." Axel stopped the car and turned to her. "You know," he went on, "you might have a much warmer instinct of sympathy for Dirk if you were in like case yourself."

"How do you mean?" (Did he but know it, she was!)

He answered slowly, "Well, as any of us may be, sooner or later. Perhaps in love, but perhaps only half committed, none too sure of our ground. Doubting whether we do love, or love enough or too much. Whether our 'she' or our 'he' really knows us. Whether we are loved at all, or a little, or equally, in return. But doubting and wondering and asking ourselves, we don't usually run to the nearest Little Miss Oracle for advice. Not a bit of it. We resort to the old-fashioned method you say Dirk was using, and we find out."

"Just by lovemaking?" Jonnet shook her head. "No, it's too – easy. It can't tell the real things, the things that matter between two people. That takes time, and getting to know. And agreeing and differing and – exploring ... all that."

"Oh, I don't know. Dirk's way is time-honoured, and pleasurable, and it wouldn't be so popular if it didn't afford some clues as to whether further exploration is likely to be rewarding. On the principle of a gramme of practice being worth a kilo of theory – you know? As, for instance, supposing you and I –? Well, supposing –"

As he broke off, took her by the shoulders and bent to her, she knew at once what the mischief of his mood intended – knew, and surrendered to the long hard pressure of his mouth on hers, her newly-realised need of his touch and his nearness incapable of resisting him while it lasted. She longed to believe it was sweetly meant and tender and revealing. But when his hands slid down her arms and stayed briefly at her wrists before he sat back, there was a devil in the blue eyes which denied it.

"Well?" he questioned. "In the way of experiment, what would you say of its merits?"

"Experiment" jarred, hardening her will. She said, "You mean, what more did it tell me than I knew before? As I expected, nothing. Except that – in that sort of thing – you are very experienced."

He laughed. "Thank you. Let's say I've made use of my – opportunities as they have offered. But don't you want to hear what it taught me about you – if anything?"

"If anything –"

"Such enthusiastic encouragement!" He laughed again. "But I admit I have to echo you and say Nothing. Except perhaps that in 'that sort of thing', though you lack flair, under tuition you might prove to be what actors call, I think, 'a quick study'. However, proficiency in that sphere wasn't really what we set out to prove, was it? It was merely a possible means to an end –"

"Which we are agreed hasn't materialised!" Jonnet took him up quickly, on the defensive now, wary. She opened the car door and got out. He joined her after lifting out her bicycle and giving it to her. As if nothing had changed – and of course for him it hadn't – he said easily, "And Amsterdam? What about a date for that?"

"Oh – Well, in fact," she evaded, "I'd rather promised Dirk that he should show it to me."

"Then we'll abandon the guided tour and take it piece-meal. Do you appreciate music? In the autumn season you can hear some of the best orchestras in the world at the Concertgebouw."

"I shan't be here in the autumn."

"Can you think of any more difficulties to make? Any-way, there is music of some sort all the year round. I'll take tickets and ring you." He made his good night a mere touch on her hand and got back into the car.

Indoors Grethe, at her knitting, was counting stitches at an armhole. Stating, not asking a question, she said, "You went out on your bicycle and you come back by car."

Jonnet said, "Yes. Axel Keyser's."

"He is back from England, then?"

"Yes. After skating I went to see Dirk. But he was — busy, and Axel gave me tea and brought me home."

"You arrived a while ago. You took a long time to bid each other good night. You should have asked him in to see me."

"I don't think he would have come. He was on his way to his farm. That's why he brought me out."

"You should still have asked him in. It would have been polite. Besides, he is a suitable man for you to know, and I am pleased that he takes an interest in you."

"That's only through his being your neighbour and be-cause I'm Dirk's sister," Jonnet pointed out.

"Showing that he sets some importance on family con-nections, which is an attitude which we Dutch value in a man. It was a pity that your father lacked it in such measure. But if Axel Keyser should look closer to home for a wife than to one of the pretty fly-by-nights he has pursued in the past, that would be a good change of heart to see."

Jonnet said a little wearily, "Well, please don't think he's considering me as a possible wife. His only interest in me is his determination that I shall learn to appreciate Holland while I'm here."

"And so? Do you never ask yourself why he should care that you should?"

Jonnet nodded. "Of course, though I suspect often that it has less to do with Holland than that he enjoys being in the right and putting me in the wrong."

"Which annoys you, no doubt?"

"When I let it, and I confess I often do. For instance, this evening we were finishing off an argument – one of our many – which was why you had to notice that I didn't leave him and come in at once."

Grethe had finished her counting and was now knitting busily. "Though it would be news to his friends that Axel Keyser was ever known to linger longer than he need with a girl merely to find fault with her," she murmured.

"Well, it was so tonight, and often has been, I assure you," said Jonnet.

There was a pause. Then Grethe addressed her clicking needles. "Yes?" she asked of them unanswerably.

CHAPTER SIX

Now the first peak of the bulb season was in sight, with the spears of the field-grown daffodils and narcissi breaking their papery sheaths and at that "pencil" stage being gathered and bunched for a market which of recent years preferred to buy and sell them so, before they opened to full bloom.

From certain of almost every holding's fields the flowers were not marketed, the parent bulbs of these being of more value when they were lifted and sold later in the season. At the Boerdery Handel most of the crop was so held back. But for a season of many days there was gathering to be done for the morning auctions at Aarlsmeer where each day's quota of blooms would begin arriving before dawn and where kilo upon kilo of cut flowers would be bidden for and disposed of to local and foreign wholesalers by the clock-auction method peculiar to Holland. And from nearby Schiphol Airport there would be the regular evening air-lift to the neighbouring capitals of Brussels and Paris and Covent Garden in London.

Jonnet, willingly enlisted into the Boerdery's small army of gatherers, enjoyed this time of early rising and busyness. At first her back had ached intolerably, but gradually she schooled it to a rhythm of stooping and gathering which she learnt from the other women workers. She never gathered as fast or as expertly as they did, but she added quite a respectable quota of fragrant bunches to the total which Munt loaded and transported to Aarlsmeer or to the florists of Amsterdam every day.

Meanwhile she waited for Dirk to confide to her anything about his involvement with Saskia. They spoke frequently on the telephone, but she deliberately asked him nothing, making of her silence a pact which Axel hadn't demanded of her but which she meant to keep. Dirk came less often to the farm at weekends or in the evenings, from which she concluded he was spending more time with Saskia, and as she had finished her course of skating lessons and hadn't booked for more, she was a less frequent caller now at the little apartment on the Herengraacht. In fact, she had seen so little of Dirk lately that she sometimes reflected how empty had been her excuses to Axel in order to evade obligation to him. With Axel rebuffed and Dirk neglectful, it looked as if she would have to explore historic and cultural Amsterdam for herself!

And then, in the end, it was not to be Dirk who offered confidences, but their Aunt Letti Moet who made a rare special journey out to the farm to blazon the news of the affair, to enlist Grethe's sympathies on her side and to accuse Jonnet fretfully of Keeping Things From Her.

Chauffeur-driven to the farm gate, Letti picked her way across the mud-trodden driveway with the air of a queen who had missed out on the services of a Sir Walter Raleigh. Disdaining the courtesy of a knock, she walked straight into the house to find her sister and Jonnet at *koffietafel*. She refused to join them, saying her diet did not allow her to eat at midday, and going straight to the matter which had brought her, accused Jonnet,

"You must have known what is going on between your brother and my darling girl. Yet you have said nothing. Why not?"

Taken by surprise, Jonnet said, "I only know what I have guessed myself, but I should have thought you might know how much they are seeing each other – from Saskia."

"I trust my girl. I do not ask everywhere she goes or

104

with whom," Letti returned loftily. "And thought I knew that Dirk would like to make a nuisance of himself, I thought she would know how to manage him."

Before Jonnet could reply to that Grethe interposed, "Given your training of her, she should know how to handle ineligible men," her dry tone showing Jonnet where her elder aunt's sympathies lay, but giving offence to Letti, who complained sadly,

"You too, then?"

"Too?" Grethe queried.

"On Dirk's side. On hers –" indicating Jonnet. "Even on Saskia's, while she chooses to encourage him, which one hopes will not be for long. Must I be the only one then to deplore this folly – this nonsense of an idea that a match between them would be suitable or even possible at all?"

"Why shouldn't it be either?" enquired Grethe. "They are much of an age. Dirk is hard-working and should go far in his profession. And for him to marry a Dutch girl would please *me* very much."

"Saskia is not fully Dutch. As you know very well, her mother was Spanish, which is why the child is so dark and dainty and, no doubt, so attractive to men. Why, she could marry anyone – anyone at all! She has money of her own from her father, and she will have all mine. And of course it can't but occur to one that Dirk knows this, and is turning it to his advantage," declared Letti.

That was too much for Jonnet. For all her own bias against the affair, she sprang to Dirk's defence. "How dare you?" she demanded. "Dirk isn't like that. He doesn't need to be. He's no penniless adventurer. If he is courting Saskia, and I think he is, it must be because he is in love with her, and if she is encouraging him –"

"Knowing Saskia, it is probably only because she enjoys collecting another scalp for her belt." That was

105

Grethe, finishing the sentence dryly, and caustic as the remark was, it seemed to afford Letti some relief.

"You think then that *she* has not lost her head? That *she* is not serious?" she hazarded.

Grethe shrugged. "Who can tell, without seeing them together? If you want to know how far the thing has gone, why do you not ask her? Or Dirk? Or both of them?"

"Not the two of them." Letti shook her head. "That would be to admit that the situation exists. As soon as found out, I did ask Saskia of course. But nowadays girls – even good ones like my Saskia – tell one nothing they do not please, and think they have a right not to do so. But as long as you know what is going on, and I have the word of both of you that you won't encourage it –?"

Upon which, apparently assuming that she had such a promise from the other two, she rose to go, saying she must not keep Fredrik waiting.

When she had gone, Grethe looked across at Jonnet. "Well, do we give her such a word or not?" she asked. And then, "How much have you known of all this, without telling me?"

"Nothing from Dirk himself."

"Then from what?"

"From guessing that he has always been attracted by her, from seeing her in his arms once, and from the little either of us have seen of him lately, while he must be taking her about."

Grethe agreed, "Yes, I have wondered about that myself. And from the way you defended Dirk to Letti, you would be pleased at such a match?"

"Not really," Jonnet admitted. "I resented Tante Letti's calling him a fortune-hunter, but I shouldn't like him to marry Saskia."

"Nor I. So that we are one of the same mind about that,"

said Grethe.

"But you told Tante Letti that you would like him to marry a Dutch girl," Jonnet remind her.

"A Dutch girl, yes. But Dutch or only half Dutch, not Saskia Moet. I only disagreed with Letti because I usually do," returned Grethe blandly. "And so we can give her our word with a clear conscience. Though our reasons are different from hers, we do not care for this nonsense any more than she does. But what to do about it? You have not told Dirk what you feel, you say?"

Jonnet shook her head. "No. At first I meant to, but I was advised – That is, I thought it wise not to, in case he turned stubborn for stubborness' sake."

Grethe pounced on her unfinished phrase. "You were 'advised'? And who advised you so?" she demanded.

"Well, Axel Keyser."

"And so you were able to agree with him for once? Enough, anyhow, to obey him?"

"In order not to antagonise Dirk, yes."

"Which was indeed wise advice. Rash and prodigal of his heritage as Axel may be – fun-fairs and carousels on good rich bulb land! – in affairs of the heart he shows diplomacy. As, with all his experience, well he may, it could be said of him. And so we wait to act, I think, until the affair reaches the point where Dirk confides his hopes or his plans to you, or to me, or perhaps to Axel. Then we shall know where we stand and what we have to fight."

"Though we can't move them about like puppets, and if Dirk really does love Saskia, things may have gone too far for us to have the right to interfere," Jonnet demurred.

"Possibly, and one must have sympathy, of course. But that is a dyke, as we say, for which we must find a bridge when we come to it." Grethe rose and began briskly to clear the table. "At least for once I shall *appear* to be in accord with Letti, and it would seem that you are with Axel on this. So that if, between us, we cannot save Dirk from disaster —" She broke off to admonish Jonnet, still seated, "Switch off the electric fire, child, when you come out. We both have work to do in the office, and there is no need to heat an empty room."

During the next week or two Dirk gave no sign of wanting to confide in Jonnet, nor did Axel implement his casual suggestion of inviting her to the Concertgebouw, although, watching the advertisements, she noticed that an orchestra from Berlin had been on tour to Amsterdam; so had a famous Vienna choir, and a visiting ballet company had danced *Swan Lake* and *The Sleeping Beauty* on successive nights. If Axel had rung up, she would have accepted eagerly, glad that her speculations as to his silence were over. She would have known that his invitation hadn't been a mere exit line, and that he hadn't taken seriously her silly rejection of his renewed offer to show her the city. But with every day when he did not ring, increasingly she decided that he did not mean to, and though she despised the vagaries of mood which swung between love and hurt pride, she indulged them both in turn, the one sweetened by the remembered thrill of his kiss, the other indignant that she should have let it happen.

It was in the spirit of her resignation to exploring Amsterdam alone that she took herself one day to the Rijksmuseum, bought a catalogue of the paintings in the foyer and took it outside into the sun, meaning, as it was impossible to cover all the galleries under several hours, to mark the whereabouts of the pictures she most wanted to see.

It was the hour of the morning exodus from every office in the city, in search of the Dutch equivalent of "elevenses" and a short breather in the spring sunshine. The pavement coffee stalls were doing good business and the seats in the gardens bordering the Stadhoudeskade were almost all full. Jonnet found a perch at the end of one of them, which emptied at last, leaving her room to move up a little and a young dark man at the far end to move down.

She glanced askance in his direction, interested in what he was doing – sketching rapidly on a drawing block, though not, it seemed, anything of the scene before him. Twice he discarded his efforts, tearing off sheets and thrusting them into a pocket, and once did not seem to hear when a passerby with an unlit cigarette between his fingers stopped to put him a question.

The man asked again. The artist looked up, echoed, "*Metsi?*" adding in an unmistakable English accent, "Oh – matches!" and producing a pack of book matches. "Here you are. Keep them. I have more." Whereupon the other man, understanding the gesture if not the words, bowed his "*Dank U, mijnheer*" and went on his way.

The dark young man met Jonnet's eye and half-smiled before pencilling again for a while and then discarding that sheet with a wholly English expletive which brought Jonnet's bent head up with a jerk.

"Sorry." He laughed self-consciously. "I believe you understood that?"

She smiled back. "Yes."

"*And* the bit with the matches chappie? I thought you seemed to be listening. You understand English well? Speak it too, perhaps?"

Jonnet smiled again. "I ought to. I am English. And so are you, aren't you?"

"As they come," he agreed heartily. "Name – Mervyn Hawke." He indicated the catalogue she held. "And you? Student? Tourist? Doing the sights?"

"Neither, really. I'm staying out at my aunt's farm in

109

the country for a while. I haven't been to the Rijks yet, and as I knew I couldn't 'do' it at one go, I was going to pick and choose."

"What are you going for? What do you like?"

"Well, the Rembrandts, of course, and Franz Hals, and any Dutch interiors, and I like Peter Breughel." Jonnet nodded at the sketch block. "You are an artist yourself?"

"Not really. I'm a freelance display man – show-window designs for department stores – that sort of thing. And it's odd you should mention Breughel, because it's an idea based on one of his winter scenes that I was working on, and it won't 'come'. It's a commission from a friend of mine. I'm staying here with him while I do the job." Mervyn Hawke paused. "I suppose you wouldn't let me do the Rijks with you? I've been here before, and I know all the best things to see."

Jonnet hesitated. "I haven't too much time –"

"Well, tell me how long and I'll ration the fare. Besides, I want another look at the Breughels myself. Shall we?"

There seemed no reason to refuse. On their way across the road he said, "You haven't told me your name. Are you going to?"

"It's Handel – Jonnet Handel."

He stared and halted, and Jonnet had to pluck him clear of a horde of cyclists. As they went on he accused, "That's not an English name. You said –" and then, "*Handel?* Now there's an odd thing. In the ground-floor apartment of my friend's place on the Herengracht there's a chap named Handel – a teacher and half English, he says."

At that a memory clicked for Jonnet – Mevrouw Bernard's telling her about Axel's friend who came each year to design the Broadlands float for the Corso. Working it out for her own and Mervyn Hawke's benefit, she said. "Then you are staying with Axel Keyser, and the Handel

110

you know is Dirk, my brother, and our names are Dutch because our father was, but I told you I was English because I think of myself so." She dimpled. "And now, who is going to say 'It's a small world' first?"

"You can," Mervyn conceded. "*I'm* going to say it's a pleasant one, letting me meet you like this, more than half-way to knowing each other. So you know Axel too, I suppose?"

Jonnet was aware that she had blushed. "Yes," she said.

"And what I'm doing here – designing his Corso thing? And of course you'd know a rather stunning brunette, perfectly put together, from her feet to her head – Saskia Moet, who's always around, about equally, I'd say, in your Dirk's place and in Axel's? Axel says she's Dirk's girl, but –"

"But what?" Jonnet's tone was sharp.

Mervyn glanced at her quickly. "Nothing. Only that Axel calls her his kitten and they chat each other up a lot, and at first I couldn't sort the three of them out. However, this isn't doing the galleries. Let's go."

They achieved an easygoing intimacy as they went round the museum, discussing the pictures. But telling him something of her own circumstances and learning his, Jonnet was aware of a small doubt at the back of her mind.

She had told Mervyn Hawke that she thought of England as her home and of herself as English as he. But was that the whole truth now? Now, since she had come to love Axel, to love Holland, both for itself and because of him? Wasn't she just a little proud now of her Dutch name, of the Dutch blood which ran in her veins, and in speaking of the farm, to call it quite naturally "home"?

They used all of the time she had allowed herself, which made it easy to refuse to go back with Mervyn to "reveal all", as he called it, to Axel or to Dirk, should either be

111

at home. She would *not*, she told herself, appear to seek Axel out. Nor Dirk, for that matter, while he held aloof from her. But when Mervyn suggested, at their parting, that they should "do" some other of the city's sights together, it seemed a good idea. He knew Amsterdam better than she did, and since she had put Axel off and Dirk seemed too preoccupied, she agreed that she and Mervyn should escort each other. They made a date, for a trip by water-bus round the harbour and through the intricate network of the canals, for two days ahead, meeting at the ticket office for the afternoon tour.

That was a success too, but at the end of it and when they had sauntered round the Singel flower market and Mervyn had bought Jonnet a little posy of forced rosebuds, he would not allow her to play Cinderella again by slipping away. Axel would be at home, he said, and he had promised to take her back. Besides, surprise, surprise! he had hired himself a bicycle and meant to ride back to the farm with her afterwards. On their way, they would discuss their next date . . .

They found Axel in his study on the second floor of the mansion, but he wasn't working. He was talking to Saskia who was perched on a corner of his desk, fashioning a winged Dutch bonnet for herself out of a sheet from his blotting pad, fastened with paper-clips. The scene was intimate to a degree and Jonnet was reminded sharply of Mervyn's alleged perplexity as to whose girl Saskia was. "Around" with Axel as often as with Dirk, was she? So what was going on? Jonnet wondered jealously.

Axel nodded to Mervyn and greeted her easily, making no excuse for having neglected to be in touch with her. Saskia finished the bonnet and put it on, giving it a backward tilt on her dark hair. She glanced provocatively at both men. "How do I look? Would you say it was utterly me?"

she enquired.

"Not at all. You look like a nurse who's run short of safety-pins. Alternatively, as if you were about to take o' into orbit," was Axel's dry comment.

"Beast!" She pulled a face at him and turned to Mervyn. "What about you?"

He shook his head too. "No. You're too dark an' soignée – not Dutch enough. Better let Jonnet try it on – with her blonde hair, she's much more of the Dutch type than you."

But flicking off the bonnet, Saskia crumpled it and threw it into the wastepaper basket. "Too bad," she said. "But I never did aspire to Dutch looks anyway. Our women tend to grow into such frumps that I'm glad I'm half Spanish. But if I'm not the Dutch type, what am I – tell?" she appealed again to Mervyn.

He considered her. "Eastern, I think. I see you being rather glamorous in a brilliant sari and hooped earrings."

"Eastern? Oh –" She looked pleased and turned to Jonnet. "And being an artist, he should know, shouldn't he? Does he compliment you like that? And wasn't it clever of you to pick him up as you did? Even if you fancied him, if he had been the complete stranger that he might have been, think of all the explanations you would have had to make!"

Jonnet said coldly, "Explanations? To whom?"

Saskia shrugged. "Well, to Tante Grethe, I'd have thought, if you wanted to take him to the farm. I know Letti wouldn't care for *me* to be quite as casual as that. But perhaps English parents aren't as particular –" Leaving in the air the implication that Jonnet was a wanton of the worst dye, and ignoring Mervyn's attempted protest of "Look here, you can't –!" she broke off and addressed Axel again.

"So that is fixed, then? We make a party for *Die Fledermaus*?"

Axel said, "I think so, if Jonnet would like to see it. I owe her the promise of an evening at the Concertgebouw. Will you come – Wednesday?" he asked Jonnet.

She forgave him. At least he hadn't forgotten, and of course he had been busy, playing host to Mervyn Hawke. She said, "Thank you, I'd like that," and Axel said to Saskia, "If you see Dirk first, will you tell him?"

"Yes –" She bit her lip. "That is, it's going to make an odd number."

"How so?"

"Well – Mervyn and Jonnet; you and I; and Dirk. I mean, I shall have to tell Dirk that you asked me first!"

Jonnet held her breath, waiting. Would Axel alter the pairings and claim *her*? Would he? But he merely said impatiently, "Nonsense. It's a party, isn't it? We just happen to be odd, and who cares?" ignoring Saskia's sulky little murmur of, "Well, people *do*. Dirk won't like being the odd one out a little bit."

There was a brief silence. It was as if they were all aware that the climate had chilled. Then Axel said briskly, "Well, you girls may make yourselves scarce as soon as you like. I want to talk to Mervyn about the Corso."

That evoked dismay from both Saskia and Mervyn. Saskia complained, "I don't have to go, do I? Dirk isn't back yet," and Mervyn said, "Now, Axel? I can't, I'm afraid. I'm going to see Jonnet home."

Axel frowned. "While I cool my heels, waiting for you to come back?"

"Sorry," Mervyn told him, and forestalled Jonnet's protest that she was quite capable of going home by herself, by putting a firm hand to her elbow. Over his shoulder he promised Axel, "I shan't dawdle on the way back. I do want to discuss the design with you." To which Axel growled, "I'd rather you didn't dawdle *either* way," and as Jonnet and Mervyn left the room, Jonnet heard Saskia say gleefully, "That's good. For if you aren't going to work, I needn't go either!" She perched again on the corner of the desk.

On the way it occurred to Jonnet that if Axel had wanted to avoid waiting for Mervyn, he could have offered to take her and her bicycle back in his estate car, as he had done on a certain afternoon which she remembered only too well. But evidently he had opted out of any further responsibility towards her, as was shown too by his failure to claim her as his partner for the opera. That had hurt more than she could say. And how *could* he, knowing what he did about Dirk and Saskia, have assumed so readily that Dirk would not resent being the odd one out of five? Knowing only as little as she did about Dirk's and Saskia's affair, Jonnet felt quite certain that he would.

It was a puzzle which was not solved by Mervyn's own question to her. Pedalling companionably beside her, he said, "You see what I mean about those three? Is Saskia Moet Dirk's girl, or is she Axel's – which?"

"She is not Axel's," said Jonnet so sharply that Mervyn looked across at her in surprise.

"You sound very sure of that. But how so? Between them, they're ditching Dirk for the evening at *Fledermaus*, aren't they?"

(Axel is ditching *me* for the evening at *Fledermaus*, was Jonnet's bleak thought.) Aloud, on the defensive for him, she said, "That seems to have been Saskia's idea. I think she gets a thrill out of playing off one man against another – even against Dirk."

"Not that she had to twist Axel's arm to partner her, I thought," commented Mervyn. "Besides, they kiss like sweethearts, for I've seen them, and Axel didn't appear to

115

mind that I had."

"Kiss? I don't believe it! He *knows* that she belongs to Dirk!" Jonnet declared hotly.

"And you're on the warpath for Dirk because he's your brother? Well, good for you," Mervyn applauded. "But if I were he, do you know what I'd do on Wednesday?"

"No? What would you do?"

"I'd find myself the snazziest doll I could rustle up. Ah yes, a redhead – a foil to both Saskia and you – and I'd make an entrance into one of the best seats in the stalls with her on my arm, and I bet I'd have both Saskia and Axel saying, 'Look – what?' in chorus!"

Jonnet pulled herself together and laughed. "Good idea. Though I doubt if snazzy redheads grow on trees for the picking in Dirk's scholastic circles."

"No, maybe not. Still. it was a thought. Anyway," Mervyn changed the subject, "at least they paired you with me, and you'll allow that, won't you? On Wednesday night I'll hire a car and come out for you. May I?"

"You needn't. Dirk could fetch me," said Jonnet.

"To play gooseberry to him and his glamour-puss, if he can produce one?" Mervyn grinned. "No, please. Let me. I'd like to. O.K.?"

But before Wednesday Dirk himself had furnished the answer to the question which had puzzled Mervyn and was harrying Jonnet with jealous doubts of Axel. He rang up, demanding that she should be in when he drove over to the farm that evening. He would take her out driving. For he had to talk to her – alone.

On hearing that he was coming and that he didn't propose to stay to supper, Grethe commented, "So now he decides to tell you all, but why does he avoid me? Though perhaps I can guess why. He thinks he can coax some sympathy from you for this foolishness of his, but knows he can hope for none from me. However, you will be able to tell me all that he tells you, and, as it happens, I need not embarrass him tonight. I have business to discuss with Axel Keyser."

"With Axel? Is he coming here?" Jonnet asked.

"No. I shall walk over to The Broadlands to meet him and the young Englishman who brought you home the other day. Axel telephoned this morning to ask my help with their project for the Corso, and though, until I had consulted Munt, I couldn't give Axel a firm answer, Munt has now agreed, and I can tell Axel I shall be glad to help."

"In what way?"

"With white tulip heads, of which we shall have available several thousand. White hyacinths they have in plenty, and white narcisci too. But they lack enough white heads in all to carry out Mijnheer Hawke's design. And therefore," Grethe added, not without pride, "they must look to my humble farm for them!"

Reflecting wryly that, without Munt's consent to the contribution, Axel might have gone a'begging for white tulips, Jonnet asked, "Why do they need so much white? What is the design this year?"

Grethe shook her head. "That I have not heard, though no doubt Axel will tell me in confidence tonight. As you know, I am not in a big enough way to send a float. But all the big holdings which do are very jealous about keeping their designs secret until they are actually being made up — lest their ideas should be stolen while there could still be time for them to be copied by another company."

"Yes, I remember Mevrouw Bernard's saying that the designs were kept very hush-hush," Jonnet agreed.

"That's so. Until the last possible minute there are just the few people who have to know, and can be trusted,"

Grethe amended, and then with a lightning switch of subject, asked, "And the Englishman, Hawke – how deep is his interest in you?"

Jonnet laughed in sheer surprise at the question. "Deep?" she echoed. "It's not deep at all. He enjoys showing me the city, I think, and I like being shown it. And he is English, which makes a nice change. But that's all."

Grethe reproved, "In four short months with us I should not have thought that you need yet be looking for a change from our own men. Goodness knows, we have fine specimens enough for your choice! However, Axel told me when you first came that he would make himself responsible for showing you such of our ways and our places of interest as you ought to have learned about from your father, but didn't. So how does Axel view your almost daily excursions now with Mijnheer Hawke – and even to the opera next, you say?"

"We are making a party for the opera," Jonnet pointed out. "And even if Axel did appoint himself as my guide at first, I can't really see what right he has to 'views' on where I go or who escorts me now."

"His right, surely, and as you've mentioned yourself, as my neighbour and Dirk's friend?" Grethe queried.

"Yes – well, it isn't as if I'd suddenly taken up with a complete stranger. Mervyn Hawke is Axel's friend too!"

"And takes advantage in consequence."

"Takes advantage? What do you mean?"

But Grethe either could not or would not say.

That night, parting from Dirk, Jonnet stood by the car and made her last appeal. "Are you quite sure that it isn't all Saskia's doing?" she asked.

Frowning, Dirk thumped the heel of each hand on the steering-wheel. "Of course I'm sure! How many more times must I tell you? It takes two, doesn't it? And Saskia *had* begun to care before Axel made this dead set at her — I know she had!"

"But if she really cared for you, should it have been so easy for Axel to get her away from you?"

Dirk growled, "That's about the fourth time you've said that. Because, I suppose, you'd like to blame Saskia rather than Axel. For all I know, he may have got you in thrall too. But all right — perhaps at first she was flattered. He's got more to offer any girl than I have, goodness knows. But it's he who has made all the running — dining her, taking her dancing — the lot."

"I still can't forget that she once taunted you that she could 'get' even him, if she wanted him," Jonnet persisted. "But how long has this been going on, did you say?"

"Long enough. About since he last came back from England."

"Which was about when I realised you were in love with Saskia and I've been waiting ever since for you to tell me about it."

"Yes, well —" Dirk hesitated. "I think I was afraid you might try to 'manage' it. You tend to, you know. And Saskia wanted to keep it secret too — from Tante Letti's interference, I suppose."

"Underrating Tante Letti's nose for a love affair of which she couldn't approve for Saskia. I was there when she came to demand of Tante Grethe that she stop it. Me, she accused of aiding and abetting."

"And she could have saved herself the trouble, couldn't she? Seems now there's nothing for her or Tante Grethe to stop, or you to aid and abet," said Dirk dejectedly. "Now we all wait for the engagement to be announced, and after that, the wedding bells."

"Unless it's just another affair of Axel's, of which people

say he has had many," said Jonnet, clutching at straws. She put her hand through the open car window and laid it on one of Dirk's. "Dirk, I'm sorry. When you wanted to see me tonight, I never expected this. I thought that at last you were going to ask me to congratulate you," she told him."

"And could you – about Saskia?"

She hesitated. "I'd have tried, I think – if you were happy about her." She paused. "Tell me, do I really try to manage too much?"

He turned his hand upward and squeezed hers. "Let's say I've got used to it by now," he offered, and managed a thin smile for her before, with a "See you!" he drove off.

In the house she found Munt, eating his supper alone in the kitchen, grumbling to no one but himself that in these days it was nothing but cars, cars, coming or going at all hours. They were better times, to his way of thinking, when folks went about their business or did their courting on foot until they could afford a bicycle, which they paid for before they got it, instead of months afterwards ... In order to escape him Jonnet collected a roll and cheese and fruit on a tray and left a note for Grethe to say that she had gone to bed early.

She wanted time too, to think before reporting to Grethe on the collapse of Dirk's romance with Saskia. Grethe hadn't wanted to hear it was flourishing and looking for people's good wishes for its future. But no more than Jonnet had, could she have expected Dirk's dire news of Axel's having deliberately and heartlessly lured Saskia away from him.

How was Grethe going to take it? Was she going to believe it, as Jonnet feared from both Dirk's and Mervyn's evidence, she would have to? As Jonnet herself must, knowing that in trying to gauge her aunt's reactions, she was only postponing the pain of facing her own.

Nothing Axel had ever said or done gave her the right to feel so utterly betrayed. But she did. He hadn't encouraged her to fall in love with him. That was her own misfortune. But she *had* believed in his honour; *had* thought she could trust his good faith. Dirk was his friend! And he had been blunt enough with her reluctance to accept Dirk's affair with Saskia to convince her that he accepted it himself. Yet even then – for Dirk had said that his pursuit of Saskia had stemmed from that day of his return from England – even then he must have planned to betray Dirk, knowing, as he surely must, that he had more to offer Saskia's self-indulgence than Dirk ever could; that against him Dirk would be competing completely out of his class.

How could he? How *could* he? her sore heart agonised. To love a man you needed to know that in a matter of honour he would act as you would have him act. If he failed that test, then by just so much he had failed you... Standing and staring from her uncurtained window, without having attempted to undress or eat anything from the tray, she was wondering bleakly whether, by showing her Axel's feet of clay, this might be fate or her good angel beginning to cure her of her need of him, when there was a knock on her door and Grethe came in.

Deflating as ever towards weakness, Grethe said, "A girl of your age shouldn't come to bed at this early hour unless she is sickening for something." She glanced at the tray. "You haven't touched your supper. Are you then feeling ill?"

"No, not at all." Jonnet sought for an excuse. "It was just that Munt didn't seem in a welcoming mood, and I didn't know what time to expect you back. So I came up."

Grethe nodded, satisfied. "And Dirk? You saw him?

What did he have to tell you?"

"That whatever there was between him and Saskia, it's broken off." Baldly, not bothering to choose her words, Jonnet added, "Axel's doing. He is courting Saskia heavily himself, and she has dropped Dirk flat."

To her surprise, Grethe registered neither astonishment, nor disbelief nor dismay nor gratification. It crossed Jonnet's mind that she might almost have known the facts already, though she hadn't known them that afternoon and it was hardly likely that Axel would have since made a boast to her of his duplicity.

Her first dry comment was, "Well, one of us at least will be pleased about that. It should be all that Letti could have asked for her darling girl."

And her second – "And *you* should have made good hay of Axel's interest in you while you had it, niece. Now it could be too late."

It was an exit line which left Jonnet speechless.

CHAPTER SEVEN

THAT night, before she slept, Jonnet remembered that she hadn't asked Dirk whether he meant to make the fifth in Axel's party for the opera, so she rang him the next day.

"Well, what do you think?" was his laconic reply.

"I know what I'm afraid to think – that you won't come," she told him.

"And how right you could be, at that."

"But I'd much rather think that you will."

"Managing me again?"

"Is that managing you – wanting you to come, without any power to make you?"

"More in sorrow than in anger, eh? Well, thanks for the well-meant persuasion, but I'll see Axel and his lopsided party further first."

"And give Saskia the satisfaction of knowing that you are hurt enough not to be able to meet her?"

"I've *had* to meet her – too often. She's always calling at Axel's place, or he's taking her out in his car, and they both go out of their way to make sure I notice."

"But have you said anything to her about it all? Or to Axel?" Jonnet worried. "Or did you just let it happen?"

"Saskia refuses to be long enough alone with me to discuss it, and I've more pride than to ask Axel to leave her alone. As his tenant I have to speak to him the necessary minimum. But if I hadn't got his wretched apartment on the rest of the year's lease, I'd get out tomorrow."

"But need you actually stay in it if you don't want to? I'm sure Tante Grethe would make room for you to come back here, and you could commute to school every day," Jonnet suggested.

There was a pause during which she thought he was considering that. But he said, "Forget it. I wasn't serious. It would look too much like running away."

Quickly Jonnet snatched her advantage. "Just as you will appear to be running away if you opt out of the party," she said. "Why don't you come, and bring another girl? You must know plenty by now."

"Of course I do."

"Well then —?" But Dirk rang off without replying.

As Jonnet got ready for the evening she remembered her social blunder at Saskia's skating party and, for the Concertgebouw, hoped she wasn't overdressing in her best long dress of gold-brown silk damask under a chocolate-brown cape and having had her hair styled at an exclusive salon in the city. Though Axel wouldn't notice, and Saskia would certainly outshine her, she had dressed, not so much for him, as to state a poise and an independence of him which at heart she could not feel. For as every girl knew, when your pride needed a boost, a sense of looking your best did help.

When Mervyn called for her, from his admiring look it seemed that he at least approved. He said ingenuously, "You know, at first glance I knew that you were a pretty girl; I hadn't realised until now that you are quite beautiful. You've got a lovely profile."

"Have I?" Jonnet smiled, pleased.

"Don't pretend you haven't been told so, dozens of times before now!"

"I don't think I have, and one's profile isn't something one knows much about, oneself."

"You're too modest. For instance, I bet Saskia Moet studies hers from every angle in a triple mirror, to judge of

124

its effect. By the way —" Mervyn broke off — "did you know that Dirk is showing the flag to Saskia by bringing a girl of his own tonight?"

"He *is*? I spoke to him on the phone the other morning, and he didn't say. How do you know?"

"Axel went over early to the Moets' for drinks. We are to meet him and Saskia and the other two in the foyer. And Dirk asked me in for a drink before coming out for you, and the girl, Gertrude Spetz, was there."

"A — a snazzy redheaded doll?"

Mervyn smiled. "A redhead, but that's all. In fact, you could say carrots without being unkind. A round face, turned-up button of a nose and the inevitable freckles that go with carrots. Very quiet. Hangs adoringly on Dirk's every word. In fact she has the air of having adored him at first sight."

"Why, how long has he known her? He has never mentioned her."

"I doubt if he was aware of her existence, female-wise, while he was involved with Saskia. She is a visiting art teacher at his school and she speaks English well, as they all seem to."

"Well, I'm glad he is bringing her, even if she isn't much competition against Saskia," said Jonnet.

"Ah, you never know," Mervyn said sagely. "There's competition and competition, and when a man is down, the sort of devotion this chick seems to have for Dirk can pour a lot of balm on the ego."

He had described Gertrud Spetz well. She was a bonny girl with few pretensions. Dirk was very attentive to and considerate of her, for which, even if he were only showing his independence of Saskia, Jonnet gave him full marks.

Evidently Gertrud and Saskia had met before, for they weren't introduced and greeted each other with nods. Saskia was incredibly ethereal in a peacock-blue sari, a tribute, she told Mervyn archly, to his appraisal of her as "Eastern". When Axel had first seen her wearing it, she said, he had remarked that the trendier chameleons could profit by taking lessons from her. And as you never could *tell* with Axel whether that was a compliment or not! – she wanted Mervyn's assurance that there was a dash of the Oriental about her nature. She had always had a suspicion there might be ...

The production and décor of *Fledermaus* were brilliant, and the opera ran its infectiously gay course to the enthusiastic enjoyment of the huge audience. Afterwards Axel's party adjourned for supper to one of Amsterdam's Indo-Chinese restaurants, where presently the talk turned to the subject of the Corso, and after the last course, before they took coffee, Mervyn demonstrated his plans for The Broadlands float on the cleared table.

"It's a skating scene." He glanced across at Jonnet. "I thought friend Breughel would inspire me some time if I stuck to him," he said. "The whole setting white – white ice-floor, banks of cleared snow surrounding it; the only colour – but that a positive kaleidoscope! – being the girl skaters' dresses in every hue that Axel's tulips and hyacinths can muster. Their partners just in plain green, I think, to act as foils, and the lot of them in tableau on the ice. And the centrepiece, the highlight – the ice queen – one girl poised alone, and she the only one in white, so that she stands out unmistakably from the rest." He sat back and looked around the others. "Well, that's the idea," he told them. "What do you think of it?"

They murmured their enthusiasm for it as an attractive idea, then began to discuss its practicalities – the need for a bluish light to throw shadows on the banked snow; the colossal number of flower-heads the scene would need;

how many pairs of skaters the area would accommodate; the choice of an ice queen.

Between them, Axel and Mervyn dealt in masterly fashion with the problems. They had foreseen the need for light and shade in the banked "snow"; if The Broadlands hadn't a big enough quota of flowers, neighbouring holdings which weren't sending a float, such as the Boerdery Handel, would help; they thought six couples on the "ice" would be enough. The ice queen – well, that question was still open, Axel said; the suggestions of the assembled company would be welcomed, but not necessarily taken.

Gertrud asked shyly, "You'll choose your cast of skaters from your staff, I suppose?"

Axel said, "That's the idea. We can boast some man-shaped men and some pretty peachy specimens from amongst our girls, and Mervyn has his eye on some likely candidates."

"But not on your ice queen yet?"

"Well, not from that quarter, I think. There's a delicate matter of enviable precedence involved, and we can't afford to hurt anyone's feelings."

"You think you might, if you chose one of them?" asked Gertrud.

"We'd rather not risk it, which we shouldn't if we chose an outsider."

Saskia's dark eyes sparkled. "Who would need to be quite a looker and also the best skater you can get?" she asked.

"M'm – not necessarily a skater. She'll be in tableau, as they all will be. None of them will move. They couldn't very well even pretend to skate on a rink that is only made of white flower-heads. No, but as you say, she must be quite a looker – and of course, a blonde."

The sparkle turned to an angry flash. "A *blonde*?" Sas-

127

kia echoed: "Why?"

Axel laughed. His finger and thumb made to pinch her cheek, a gesture from which she jerked away. "Sorry, my kitten, if you had ambitions," he laughed again. "This happens to be a Dutch scene, and our prejudice runs in favour of blondes. So unless you go in for a heavy course of peroxide, I'm afraid you don't qualify. As a looker – yes, every time. But as a Dutch-bonnet type, doing her stuff – no." He paused and looked round the table. "Now – saving any better ideas, Mervyn and I have been thinking in terms of – Jonnet."

"*Jonnet?*" Saskia's echo came out as a shrill scream, and Jonnet herself sat back with a little gasp. Ignoring Axel, Dirk looked straight at Mervyn to comment, "Grand idea. Yours?"

Mervyn said, "No. Axel's, in fact, though I –"

Saskia cut in, "But Jonnet isn't Dutch, and as she doesn't skate, she probably couldn't hold a skating pose." She turned to Jonnet in false apology. "I'm sorry, and of course you must be flattered, but even you must see that to accept wouldn't be fair on a real Dutch girl, and that if you couldn't carry it off, you would let the whole scene down?"

Jonnet was only human. She disliked Saskia fully as much as the other girl patently disliked her, and the fact of Saskia's jealousy was enough to quell her doubts as to her rightful claim to the role. Besides, if it were really true that Axel had chosen her –! But before she could reply, Axel was saying firmly,

"Jonnet is as Dutch as you are, my pet, and at least she had the cunning to come about as blonde as we Hollanders are made. What's more, believe it or not, we have shamed her into learning to skate. And so –!" Both hands spread and his wide blue eyes challenging, he invited the table to take the matter as settled.

Mervyn said mildly, "It occurs to me that we could have asked Jonnet if she was willing," and Jonnet said, "If you think I'd be suitable, I'd love to try." But Axel was not listening. He was attending to Gertrud, who was saying diffidently, "I don't know if you'll need any help with the costumes or anything, but I've done that sort of thing for amateur dramatics at one of the schools I visit, and I'd willingly do what I could."

Axel said, "Good girl. Let Dirk know when you are free, and we'll call on you. Jonnet, we'll have a bit of a rehearsal – positions and poses – as soon as Mervyn has the framework in place. Then, when we are ready for the real set-up, *everyone* lends a hand. Understood? And" – his glance went round the table again – "I daresay I needn't remind you that there is to be no gossip, no dropped hints as to what we're up to this year? It's a code that is honoured throughout the industry – no careless talk until the show is ready to go on. It's kept strictly under wraps until then."

"Then I'm surprised you think you can afford to share the precious secret with so many of us – outsiders." Saskia made a sneer of the last word.

"Are you, kitten dear?" said Axel with cool interest. "And yet, do you know, I've always found I could trust my friends?"

There was a floor show of Indonesian dancing which they stayed to watch. The dancing was sinuous and exotic, but Jonnet found the wailing music monotonous and discordant and as if in self-defence against it, her mind wandered, shutting it out.

Would Dirk think her disloyal for having fallen in as she had with Axel's plans? No, probably not, for she remembered that to Mervyn at least, he had applauded the idea – because it was a score against Saskia, Jonnet supposed. Her thoughts off at a tangent, she realised she was puzzled by

Axel's manner with Saskia. This was the first time she had seen them together since their affair was confirmed, as it were, and whatever his fascination with Saskia, it didn't seem to have curbed his caustic tongue. But that was Axel, of course. He said what he thought, and even Saskia was no more immune than she herself had been while he – Well, during all the time when he had seemed to care to be with her, even going out of his way to look her up; a time that was over now, and wouldn't come again.

Their party broke up at about midnight. Both Dirk and Axel had been able to leave their cars near by; Mervyn had had to park his further away, and as it was raining he went alone to fetch it. Dirk and Gertrud went off; Axel unlocked his car and put Saskia into the passenger seat and then, instead of joining her, closed the door and returned to stand with Jonnet under cover.

"You needn't wait. Mervyn can't be long," she said.

"Long enough to expose you to the perils of the night."

"What perils? There are plenty of people about."

"I'm still waiting with you. Besides" – he threw her a sidelong glance – "don't pretend you haven't promised yourself a few minutes of plain speaking with me."

"I? Plain speaking? What about?"

"About my having beaten Dirk in the Saskia stakes, of course. What else?"

"As if I thought you would listen to any criticism from me about that!" she scorned.

"Which still wouldn't prevent your longing to carve me up," he retorted with shrewd truth. "So now is your chance. Go ahead. Traitor? Snake? What else have you called me under your breath? Though I could claim, you know, that you have only yourself to blame."

Her stare at him was hostile. "Blame myself for what, if you please?"

"Don't you remember telling me of Saskia's hint that if she laid a charm net for me, she could expect to catch me in it? Well, as a normal male of the species, I happen to prefer to do my own hunting and to make my own kill. So how do you know that wasn't enough to set me tipping my sharpest arrows with love-potions?"

Jonnet gasped. "You mean you –? You deliberately, and in cold blood, set about taking your friend's girl away from him, just to – to prove your cave-manhood to yourself and to her?" She drew a long, long breath of would-be disbelief. "You did *that* to Dirk simply out of – no, not even out of pride; merely out of offended pique?"

Axel didn't take up the challenge of that. He said, "What did I tell you? You've been spoiling for this moment, and a kettle that is on the boil has to spit steam. But take it a little easier, will you? I only said I *could* claim that as my motive for pursuing young Saskia. I didn't say it was."

"Then why let me think it may have been?"

"Perhaps to test your reaction, supposing I admitted to other reasons which you might see as equally ignoble."

"Well, you've had my reaction, haven't you? You know what I think."

He nodded. "I do indeed. You make it very clear that I can expect no shrift from you. Not even if I confessed to finding I was in love with Saskia and couldn't help myself."

Jonnet felt as if something had died within her. With an effort – "That would be different," she said.

"You would forgive me that?"

"I'd try. People can't help falling in love. But it doesn't excuse the way you've treated Dirk. You *and* Saskia. She hasn't even had the decency to ask him to stand aside in your favour."

"Why should she, when I haven't declared myself yet?"

Turning the knife-blade in her own wound, "But you are

131

going to?" Jonnet asked.

Axel laughed. "The examining counsel shouldn't lead the witness! May I merely admit that the situation between Saskia and me is still fluid? Progressing, but so far unresolved."

"Which amounts to telling me that it is no business of mine?"

"More or less, though you have always made Dirk's business yours, haven't you? What I really meant was that at this juncture I'm not putting you in the Axel-Saskia picture, nor explaining why I felt justified in taking Saskia away from Dirk – if she would come."

"It seems to me," Jonnet snapped, "that, having fallen for her, you saw that as justification enough. What other motive did you need? And how far did you look for one?"

"You'd be surprised. I suffered some qualms in the process."

"I doubt it. And anyway, she came, didn't she? What did you expect?"

"That."

"What do you mean – That?"

"That she would come. If only out of curiosity, since, if nothing else, Saskia is all woman – as I think I have mentioned to you before?"

"At the same time as you told me I was tiresomely top-heavy in other directions," Jonnet confirmed.

"So I did. *And* that you lacked finesse, which happens to be rather important to the matter under dispute," he countered.

"Finesse? What has finesse got to do with it?" she echoed, bewildered.

He shook his head. "Having none, you couldn't be expected to know," he said, and then looked beyond her to Mervyn's approaching car. As it stopped and he went to open the door for her he said, "I'm not the only one to have switched horses in midstream. Beware the undercurrents, won't you?" and slamming the door, gave her no chance to reply.

Now the fields of every holding in the area were no longer brown but veritable seas of colour – the yellows of late daffodils, the scarlets, whites, purples, golds and parti-shades of the tulips, and the creams, blues and rose-pinks of the hyacinths.

It was the high season for the visitors who came at the weekends in cars and for the tourists who came by the coachload on any day, to view the dazzling scene before the inevitable deheading of the blooms in the interest of the bulbs from which they sprang. Axel's lido, unfinished though it was, was a popular picnic rendezvous. People often called at the Boerdery Handel to ask the way to it, and on fine days the road which gave open access to it would be lined with parked cars, bumper to bumper.

There were the usual seasonal hazards expected in the region – cutting spring winds before which the crop shuddered and bowed while they lasted, and one or two days of vicious hailstorms which battered and decapitated some of the delicate heads. And small scandals for gossip – of someone's unfairly dismissed employee, and of someone else who was not paying his labour the proper union rate. And news of Lysbet Bernard's father having fallen from a tractor, suffering fractures to ribs and an arm which would keep him off work until after the Corso. And everywhere there was talk of the Corso itself – the need for fine weather before it and on the day, and speculation as to which concern would take the prizes this year.

Whenever she was free Jonnet walked through the fields, still feeling her sentimental care for the flowers which

133

would die their necessary death so soon now. She had bought a small camera in order to snap them in colour, so that when she was back in England she could enjoy them again. They would be a part of this interlude which she could bear to remember, when so much of the rest she would have to forget.

Walking alone, she found herself rehearsing retorts to that parting shot of Axel's about her having switched horses in midstream. Of course he was accusing her of accepting Mervyn Hawke's escort instead of his own. But whose fault was that? she wanted to demand of him. Who had promised to "educate" her, and hadn't bothered, once he had come under Saskia's spell? Who had promised (or threatened) that he would teach her to love Holland for itself, hinting at ways in which he would do it, yet now didn't seem to care whether she loved it or not? Promises, threats, hints – all as empty and meaningless as – well, as his kisses. And what would she have seen of Holland by now – the ambition of the Ijlsmeer, the quaintness of Marken, historic Arnhem – if she hadn't shared them with Mervyn, good companion Mervyn of the even temper, with whom she never quarrelled? "As you and I always do," she concluded her mental argument with Axel while, that particular afternoon, she stared with unfocussed eyes at the sea of white tulips about her.

Stared – and then suddenly, not unseeingly, but fixedly at something unexpected, strange, alien to the white expanse – a little way in from the path she was using, a single tulip head that was peachy-pink in colour, its rosy flush so widespread on the petals that the white it did show was subservient to it.

True, these Murillos, as she knew them to be, were not as pure white as they appeared in the mass. They all had a faint tingeing of pink to their double flowers. But they were

134

mainly white, whereas this one — Treading carefully between the rows, she stepped over to look down into its frilly cup. "You're a *pink* Murillo," she addressed it aloud. "Nothing but a freak – d'you know that?"

A freak. The word rang a bell. A "sport", the bulb-world called it. Almost every species threw them from time to time, and through the centuries hundreds of variations of colour, shape and growth pattern had been patiently evolved from them. And equally, as Jonnet had learned from Grethe, hundreds of apparent sports had failed to hold their difference from their fellows even into their next flowering.

So had she discovered a true sport or not? Obviously no one could say. But somebody must be told as soon as may be. For supposing it *were* – Heady with excitement, feeling a kinship with whoever-it-was who had shouted "Eureka" from his bathtub, Jonnet hurried back to the farm and found in Grethe a cautious recipient of the news.

"It could possibly be of value. Or possibly not. More than likely not, which five to seven years from now should prove. But meanwhile, Munt must be told," she ruled.

"You tell him, Tante Grethe. He won't listen to me," Jonnet demurred.

"Nonsense. It is you who have seen it, not I. And I am not tramping the Laag Veld in search of it, just because you are afraid of Munt."

"I'm not afraid of him, but I can do and say nothing right where he's concerned."

"And you are not alone in that. He can put *me* in the wrong whenever he chooses, but you should have learnt by now that I do not let it worry me. So go along and tell him of your find. I heard him come in just now. But do not tell him I wish him to let you show it to him. And you, child, do not urge it either. For one must not appear to impose one's will upon Munt. It pays always to allow that his is the best and only way to any decision. Even –" Grethe added with the vestige of a wink – "when one knows it is not!"

Munt was washing his hands at the kitchen sink and did not turn at Jonnet's bald announcement of, "There is a pink bloom growing among the Double Early Murillos on the Laag Veld." Continuing to soap wrists and elbows, "All the Murillos on the Laag Veld carry some pink," he said.

"But this one *is* pink; all over pink. No, not quite, but more pink than white."

"And what of it?"

"Well, it was different enough to make me wonder if it could be what you call a sport. And my aunt thought you ought to –" Remember diplomacy, Jonnet corrected herself. "That is, we thought you might be interested. But it is probably not important at all."

"Or it is not a Murillo, but another variety planted among them by mistake."

"Yes, of course. I hadn't thought of that." But as Jonnet turned away he halted her with a word, "Wait."

He reached for a towel and dried his hands. "On the Laag Veld, you say? Where?"

"At a spot about five rows in from the main path."

"You could take me there now? Yes? Then come."

On their way through the house they encountered Grethe who feigned surprise at their errand. "Just the child's fancy that she has discovered a sport. As if it would have escaped you!" she flattered Munt, who stumped past her, growling, "When I have finished work for the day, my time is my own, and if I choose to waste it on a wild goose chase, what's that to anyone, I'd be glad to know?"

But as they trudged over to the Laag Veld, a couple of fields away, he gratified Jonnet with a few gruff remarks and questions – almost the first non-hostile exchange with

136

which he had favoured her. And when in quiet triumph she halted and pointed – "There!" he allowed himself an interested if non-committal "Hmph."

He stepped over to the bloom and examined it for so long that Jonnet ventured at last, "It is different, isn't it? But it is a Murillo? Could it be a sport, do you think?"

Munt straightened and came back to the path, where he continued to study the freak. "A Murillo, yes. The shape is right, and it has thrown many sports in its time – yellow, purple, red, so many that they are not all cultivated any longer. A peach-pink Murillo – that would not be unusual, though of interest to me –yes."

"You are glad I drew your attention to it? What will you do about it now?"

He ignored her plea for some praise. "I shall mark it and deal with it myself when the crop is lifted."

"Only mark it? Aren't you going to take it up and separate it from the others?"

Munt looked his scorn of this suggestion. "And check it in mid-growth? No, it will be lifted with the others, when it will have formed its new bulblets, and it is these which I shall grow on and watch."

"Without knowing for years whether it is a true sport of not?"

Now Munt's glance was as pitying as it was scornful. "You do not know much about bulb-growing if you expect results overnight," he said.

"Oh, I don't, but –" As they returned to the house Jonnet was reflecting that in five to seven years no one, least of all Munt, was likely to report to her the progress or reversion of "her" bulb. One day there might – or might not – be a peach-coloured Murillo which would hold and pass on its colour. But she would not be there to see.

However, when they parted, Munt surprised her by

137

growling, "You asked me once about my Boss of Gold. That was a narcissus sport which I have grown on for three seasons now. Next year perhaps I may know what it is worth as a variety."

Jonnet said, "Yes. Mijnheer Keyser told me about it; the trouble you have taken with it."

"Ah – trouble, what is that?" Munt dismissed his labour of love with a snort. "I have taken seeds from it too, for crossing, and that is a still longer task and perhaps beyond my time. But I have made notes, records, and I could explain them to you, if you have interest enough."

Gratified beyond measure, Jonnet said eagerly, "Thank you. I should like that." And though he backpedalled at once with, "Yes, well – when I am not so busy," she felt that if he had not forgiven her as an interloper, at least he tolerated her presence. It was a chasm she had never expected to cross.

A few days later an army of casual labour moved in on the farms of the region and the de-heading process went into full swing. Such holdings as had access to canals carried the crop away by barge; on the smaller farms it was loaded into tumbrils and carted to the cover of the open barns where the floats which would be competing in the Corso were being set up.

The workers, backs bent, secateurs busy, moved with regimented speed along the rows. Behind them colour disappeared as if it had been swallowed, and the denuded fields reminded Jonnet of the forlorn look of a flock of shorn sheep – made naked for their own summer comfort, as were the bulbs for their future good.

Like everyone else on Grethe's farm, she was busy daylong, sometimes taking a hand with the cutting – when she felt she ought to apologise to every axed head, "This hurts

138

me more than it hurts you", sometimes carrying panniers of free lager for the workers' elevenses, sometimes making one of a chain, returning empty skeps for reloading. On the last few evening before the Corso she went over to The Broadlands to help in the making of Mervyn's float.

He had erected a big platform on the floor of Axel's largest lorry with removable sides and back. The banked "snow" was being painstakingly built up on its foundations, and the "ice rink" of white blossoms was being laid. Gertrud Spetz had designed and made the foundations of the skaters' costumes – jump-suits for the men, and bodices and stiffened ballet skirts for the girls, and Dirk drove her over each evening to superintend with Mervyn their completion in the rainbow colours he had envisaged, and the pure white of tulip and hyacinth heads for Jonnet's dress and bonnet. The work was planned to reach its peak of busyness on the last evening before the Corso, when the tableau would have its dress rehearsal and Axel would issue final instructions for the early morning muster and start the next day. Everything was ticking over; there were voluntary helpers by the score; the weather promised well, and then – the major scandal broke.

The Boerdery Handel, pressed by its own affairs, knew nothing of it until Jonnet, making her usual evening visit to Axel's place two days before the Corso, was told the news by Gertrud.

"The men are discussing it for the hundredth time," Gertrud said. "But of course at this late stage there is nothing they can do."

"The men?" questioned Jonnet. "Discussing what?"

"Mijnheer Keyser and Mijnheer Hawke. Dirk couldn't bring me out this evening, so I came with them. But do you mean you haven't heard what has happened? Dirk knows, and I thought he would have told you?"

139

Jonnet shook her head. "Not a thing. Something bad? About the display? The Corso? What?"

Getrud continued to stab tulip heads into buckram. "Not as bad as it might have been, but bad enough and horrible for all of us. Someone who has known what The Broadlands display is to be gave the news away to Het Bloemkwekery, one of the other competitors – in an anonymous letter, sent early enough for them to act on it if they chose."

"To act on it?" echoed Jonnet, not fully understanding the implication.

"To copy our display, or outdo it – which they could well do. Het Bloemkwekery is one of Mijnheer Keyser's chief rivals, a big syndicate, and the last people he would surely want to be betrayed to. And you see what it means, don't you?"

"Yes ... yes," Jonnet said slowly. "Someone or other who was in the secret has broken the code that Axel told us was almost sacrosanct between the competing firms. But who did know – apart from those of us who were at his party, the night the design was decided? Because none of us would have –"

"But that's just it!" Gertrud broke in. "As soon as Mijnheer Hawke began to set up the framework, most of the workers here had to know, and though they are used to having to keep the secret every year, don't you see that they – and we – are all involved? All of us, without exception, under suspicion?"

"But Axel can't possibly think –!"

"Sorry, but he has to." Unwittingly Jonnet had raised her voice in protest, and it was Axel himself, appearing at the door of the barn, who answered. He came over to them. "I gather you are discussing our latest happening?"

Jonnet nodded. "Yes, Gertrud has been telling me. But

I can't believe –! With us you made it a point of honour, and surely none of your own people would have done it, against their own interests?"

Axel agreed unsmilingly, "M'm. Reasonable thinking, but not in line with the facts. An anonymous letter was composed and sent by anyone of upward of fifty people, counting the office staff, the outside workers and my – friends. And you can't get away from that."

"But how did you hear of it?"

"From the people who received it, Het Bloemkwekery."

"They told you about it? Though why only now? Gertrud says it was sent some time ago."

"The Director was away, and his underlings left it for him to deal with. He sent it back to me, saying that the information it contained was of no interest to them, but I would probably like to see it." Axel added dryly, "In matters of business, some of us are gentlemen, you see, and Het Bloemkwekery are big enough in the industry to scorn to resort to espionage. Rather a pity that Mijnheer – or Mevrouw – X didn't realise that. They might have saved themselves.their trouble."

"But it is the slur that counts," said Gertrud quietly. "Your not knowing who could have done it, putting us all under suspicion while you *don't* know."

"But there must be some clue somewhere," Jonnet worried. "How was it done? Written? Typed? And what did it say?"

"It described our design and plans in detail – colour, tableau, the lot. It was made up of words cut from a newspaper – tedious work, that – what a waste! And it added a hopeful hint that payment for the information, sent to a newspaper box number, would not be unwelcome."

"Then doesn't that narrow it down to someone who was in need of money?"

141

"Who isn't?" Axel remarked rhetorically. "Anyway, it was a pretty futile gesture as it turned out, and whether the motive was a personal grudge, greed or just a sick joke, I may never know."

"But as you came in just now, you took Jonnet up, saying you had to suspect everyone," Gertrud reminded him. "And it is that which – well, leaves a nasty taste in the mouth."

"Yes, doesn't it?" he agreed. As if, thought Jonnet as he left them, while his doubts remained with him, he didn't mind what sourness they left in anyone's mouth.

CHAPTER EIGHT

THE whole region was en fête for the Corso, and all the anxious ears attuned to the weather forecasts were encourraged to hear that the cloud of the morning was likely to break before noon, giving sunshine over the whole area for the rest of the day.

The Broadlands float had been sent to the muster point south of Lisse before dawn. Everyone concerned in the manning of it followed later by car, and all its loyal supporters went by whatever transport they owned or could share to such vantage points as would afford the best view of the cavalcade on its fifteen-kilometre route through Lisse to the national botanical gardens of the Keukenhof between Lisse and Hillegom. In common with all the Broadland's neighbours, everyone connected with the Boerdery Handel turned out – except Munt who, grumbling his scorn of such time-wasting nonsense, stayed behind alone. Mervyn Hawke drove over to escort Grethe and Jonnet. Axel had gone ahead with the float.

It was a school holiday and at the muster point Gertrud driven from the city by Dirk, was ready to help Mervyn to dress and set the tableau – the men skaters in green, their partners in half a dozen brilliant tulip colours, and Jonnet in the white which Mervyn's design had envisaged for her.

Before she climbed on to the float to take her pose Gertrud stood back to admire her own handiwork. "There! She is ready. How does she look?" she asked Mervyn, who was standing by with Axel.

"As bonny a Dutch lass as I hoped she would," he said and, stooping, saluted Jonnet with a light kiss on her lips. She blushed and started, and to cover her embarrassment

143

held out her hand to him. "Help me up, will you?" she said. "These skates—"

But it was Axel who intervened. Ignoring her hand, he said to Mervyn, "Sorry. My casting. My privilege," and lifted her bodily in his arms, setting her on the float and stepping up himself.

"Take care! Take care! You will crush her costume," Gertrud had squealed in alarm while he held her. But the moment or two of that had passed, and now she was taking the skating pose she had rehearsed, on the little flower-covered dais apart from the other "skaters".

Mervyn and Axel stood back, surveying her. "You can drop that arm a little, Jonnet," Mervyn advised. "You are going to find it a strain after a time."

"Nonsense," objected Axel. "As a skater she is using her arms as much as her feet. Dangling it like that makes her look like the Dying Swan. So up with it again, Jonnet – come!"

"She has to hold the pose for a long while. She must be reasonably comfortable, man," Mervyn demurred.

"Who says she must?" Axel retorted. "She is an ice maiden, isn't she? And they have no feelings. So come along, Mejuffrouw Isjberg – get those arms high and winging. You're a 'flight, practically airborne, going places on your skates – Yes, so!"

"So?" he repeated to Mervyn, who nodded, "Yes, fine." They both appraised her clinically for another minute or two, Gertrud flicked a loose flower from her skirt and smiled *Tot ziens*, the Dutch "See you soon", and then they left her, their next rendezvous to be in the Keukenhof after the judging. Or so Jonnet expected until, after a long delay, during which people had relaxed their poses and had sat down gingerly on the "ice", Gertrud came back to her and sat down too.

"It is taking longer than it should to get the floats in line," she explained. "The front band is missing one of its drummers, and the back one, a cornet-player. But they should be able to move off soon." She sat forward, hugging her knees. "I have enjoyed all this so much. I am going to miss it when it is over, aren't you? And Dirk has been so good to me. I'm grateful to him for pretending that he isn't in love with Saskia Moet any longer and that he really likes being with me. Because, even though it can't be true, I think it is wonderful of him to be so kind. Don't you?"

Jonnet doubted it. "Kind?" she echoed. "No, not a bit – if it isn't true. But how do you know it's not?"

Gertrud laughed shortly and pulled at a strand of her sandy hair. "Well, look at me," she invited. "I was around all the time he was chasing Saskia, and I might as well have been invisible. And dumb. And deaf, for all he cared. And as I know he only invited me to that party for the opera because Saskia was going with Mijnheer Keyser, I do admire him for keeping it up, just not to hurt my feelings. He has even suggested that we meet in London when he goes to England for Whitsun." At Jonnet's look of surprise she added, "Oh, aren't you going too?"

Jonnet said, "I hadn't planned to, and it's the first I've heard of his going. Or yours, for that matter."

"Yes, well, he hadn't said anything to me until I told him I had been invited to stay with some English cousins for the Whitsuntide week. Then he said he had thought of going too, and couldn't we meet while we were both there," Gertrud explained.

Curiouser and curiouser, thought Jonnet in quotation marks, though of course refrained from saying so aloud. For she too had been surprised by the continuing association after Gertrud had served Dirk's purpose as a foil for Saskia for that one evening. And now, without even mentioning

145

them to her, plans for a jaunt to London and a rendezvous with Gertrud there! Was it possible, she wondered, hoping so, that Dirk had already resigned himself to Saskia's desertion; coming back to his senses at last, and that with the help of someone as likeable and intelligent and obviously as devoted as Gertrud was? Just about as soon as I can corner him to ask him, I will, Jonnet resolved – and then checked herself.

"Managing" him, Dirk had called that. "Standing on him", Axel had accused her. So she *wouldn't* utter a word about Gertrud until he confided in her, and for the moment confined herself to telling Gertrud warmly that she hoped the Whitsun project would come off.

Then there was increasing bustle about them as the procession ushers at last got the cavalcade on its way. Gertrud departed; Jonnet took up her pose, as did the rest of the tableau characters, and the floats rolled into and through the crowd-lined streets of Lisse. And after that until the Keukenhof Gardens were reached, the day belonged to the loyal admiring people whose ecstatic "Oohs" and "Aahs" at each new display became almost a continuous sound.

For Jonnet, who had not visited it before, the Keukenhof was a miracle of colour and sunlight and dappled shade and sparkling lake-water. Of course its paths and lawns were packed too with people. But on this magical spring day they were part of its gaiety and colour; it would not have been as enchanting without them.

There was a long interval before the judging; time for picnic meals and ices and time for the human element of the various displays to relax and ease its stiffened limbs. For a while the Broadlands party joined up again with, now, Saskia and her stepmother as additions to it – rather unexpectedly to Jonnet, who had supposed and hoped that Saskia's resentment might make her boycott the affair, as it

146

had done all the preparations for it. But as her Tante Letti made clear to Jonnet when they were briefly alone together, it didn't do, not to be seen along with "everyone" at such an occasion as the Corso, and that she herself had no reason for grievance against Axel. Such an *attractive* pair as he and Saskia made! And such an excellent match for her darling girl; Axel Keyser, so utterly worthy of her in every way! No, nothing was settled yet. But that could only be Saskia playing the minx a little, to punish him for all his earlier flirtations. And why shouldn't she, when it was quite obvious that he was her *slave*?

Even that exchange, cloud though it was on Jonnet's day, was to be dispersed in part when, at the judging, the Broadlands' display took second place to the First Award which went to Het Bloemkwekery for a magnificently executed reproduction of Rembrandt's painting in the Rijksmuseum, *The Night Watch*; the third place going to a children's tableau of well-known television characters. When the results were announced, everyone – prizewinners, losers and rivals alike – seemed to be kissing or embracing or shaking each other by the hand, and Jonnet happened to find herself at Axel's side when the director of Het Bloemkwekery came to congratulate him on his win.

"More of the same to you," Axel told him. "But you shouldn't get too confident. Last year we were third; this second. You have been warned; we have first prize in our sights for next!"

The other man laughed. "Just try and beat us!" he taunted, then added seriously, "I've been meaning to ask you – have you tracked down your industrial spy yet? The one who thought he could sell your scheme to us?"

Axel shook his head. "Not yet."

"You must have some idea? Some clue?"

"Ideas, yes. No proof."

"But you will keep on the trail?"

"What do you think?" Axel returned shortly, making it a statement, not a question, as they parted.

In fact, Jonnet had not to wait beyond that evening for Dirk's confidences. Back at Broadlands a buffet supper had been laid on and when she went to the table to choose some food, she found him beside her, also alone.

"Where is Gertrud?" she asked, surprising herself by her assumption that they would be together.

Dirk said, "She isn't here. She met some friends from The Hague, and they asked her to have supper with them. They were going to see her home. Are you paired up with anyone? Where are you sitting?"

"Nowhere yet."

"Then let's eat together. What would you like from here?"

She told him her choice and he brought it and his own to a table for two. As he sat down he queried, "Surprised that I could bring myself to accept Axel's hospitality and eat his food?"

"I had supposed you would be bringing Gertrud back, so I hadn't thought about it. But now you have come alone when you needn't – yes, I do wonder," Jonnet told him.

Dirk bit appreciatively into a double-decker sandwich of bacon and smoked sausage. With his mouth full, "Had an idea you might. Want to know why?" he asked cheerfully.

"May I have a guess?"

"Go ahead."

"Well, as I doubt whether, lately, you've been willing to accept anything from him, could it be that you don't bear him the same grudge as you did – over Saskia, I mean?"

Dirk nodded. "Good thinking – except that it doesn't go far enough. To wit, I haven't merely forgiven the man. I'm

148

heartily grateful to him for relieving me of the little monster before I got any more deeply involved with her. And you can believe that or not, as you please."

"I'm only too glad to believe it – if it's true and permanent."

"It's both, I assure you. And as I can almost hear you thinking, 'Pretty swift about-face, that', and 'Why?', shall I tell you why?"

"Do."

"Well, it's the salutory lesson I've learned from the way she dropped me, hot brick, the moment he showed her there was a chance of getting *him*. If she could do that once as – as wantonly as she did, even if I got her back from him, she could do it again . . . and again, with any more attractive or richer man who crossed her path. And so, though I have agonised a bit, it's curtains for Saskia Moet as far as I'm concerned. The proverbial barge-pole, and all that." Dirk paused. "But how did you guess I'd seen the light of reason?"

Jonnet said, "From Gertrud, who doesn't let herself believe you have. She is merely abject with gratitude to you for going on seeing her still when, to her thinking, you needn't."

Dirk stared. "How do you know that's what she thinks?"

"She told me so this afternoon, and wouldn't take it from me that it could be because you wanted to. She maintains you're just being kind."

"*Kind?*" he exploded. "The little muggins! The – the *darling* little muggins, if she thinks any man would be as kind as all that!"

"As all which?" Jonnet prompted innocently.

"Oh, you know – oncoming with dates, making more, monopolising as far as he can, wanting to know, wanting to tell, kissing again because he's enjoyed the first time – And

149

for pity's sake, why does she think I'm going to England at Whitsun, if not because she's going, and I want to see her there?"

Jonnet explained, "Kindness piled on kindness is how she sees that. But mind you, I don't know what she *hopes*. All she let me see was that you're out-and-out her favourite man."

"Well, she'd better be hoping the same as I am from the English happening," Dirk said darkly, then quietened to ask, "You do like her, Jonnet? You could face the idea of her as a sister-in-law?"

"Glad to. I think she's a poppet. But would it be in order to ask what *you* see in her – after Saskia?"

Dirk confessed, "It's on the total rebound from Saskia that I'm able to see just what I want in Gertrud, I think. The differences, I mean. In the way of looks, her chubby face, her carrots, her silly nose. And her sweet temper and her humour and her brains; and – well, call it modesty, if you like to be so corny. Not playing hard-to-get, but needing to be wooed, as I mean to woo her – old-fashioned word, that – once we're in England."

"You aren't saying anything to her until then?"

"No, and don't you throw out any well-intentioned hints either," he warned.

"As if I would!" Jonnet denied, though conscious of how short a time ago she would have done just that. "Paving the way for Dirk", she would have called it.

"I don't know. I wouldn't put it past you, if you thought you could do either Gertrud or me a fistful of good. But I'm handling this on my own. I want her to see me in England and England in me, if I make myself clear? She has got to realise what marrying an Englishman would be like; what marrying *me* would involve, when I'm not teaching in Holland, as I shan't be, all my life. I want to show her a

150

bit of England, hoping she'll love it. Rather as I wanted you to love Holland when I persuaded you to come over. And you do feel a bit kindlier towards it now, don't you?"

Jonnet met his anxious eyes frankly. "Much kindlier," she agreed. "I misjudged it. It's got something. In a way it's a bit like your Gertrud – not exotically beautiful, but cosy and good-tempered and sort of – wholesome. The Dutch have a word for it themselves, but I can't remember what –"

"*Gezellig*, do you mean?" Dirk offered.

"That's it – *gezellig*," Jonnet nodded, and remembered with a pang who had once used it to her and when. It had been old Mevrouw Bernard, joining with Axel to "sell" their country to her . . . Mevrouw Bernard, so practical and bright in everyday things, but old in the wisdom which knew all that the young had to learn about love with pain. Mevrouw Bernard, who had known and warned that it was possible to be most hurt by someone you loved; possible to wound deepest someone who loved you. Mevrouw Bernard, recognising in Jonnet's resentment of Axel a pattern of loving which she had not then admitted to herself –

She jerked away from her thoughts to answer the question which Dirk had asked twice.

"Axel – welcome to Saskia?" she echoed it. "Yes, I suppose he is," she said, making the careless agreement a mask for all the rebellion and cruel jealousy in her heart.

The Corso might have come and gone, but the cloud of suspicion which it had occasioned was prevented from passing by the gossip which continued to make much of it and by the Broadlands' wounded pride in its good repute; a pride which was only too ready to enlarge and invent and even to accuse.

As far as Jonnet knew, no one but Axel and Mervyn had

actually read the text of the anonymous letter, but by some mysterious clairvoyant means, everyone claimed to know its contents by heart.

Disgraceful! Unheard of! Who could have been so base? And the various pockets of thought answered that question each in its own way.

It must have been some outside enemy of Axel's. Or more likely, one should look among any strangers who might think wrongly that Het Bloemkwekery would have been agog for the secret information. Or it was someone nearer home but equally ignorant, who was in need of the reward for which he had hoped in vain. Or – among the more tolerant folk – the whole thing had been a practical joke which had misfired.

But as Gertrud had predicted, the slur remained to besmirch the blameless while the truth was not known. As Jonnet was to learn from Grethe, indignant for the reputation of her friends.

"What do you think they are saying now?" she demanded of Jonnet one morning on her return from the neighbourhood post-office. "Mevrouw Koetle from the Mill, and Astrid Huys behind the counter – each with her head close against the grille, yap-yap, nod and chatter, and neither of them caring that I stood by while one of them said it and the other agreed – that without doubt it was Berik Bernard who composed and sent the letter to Het Bloemkwekery!"

"Lysbet's father? Mevrouw Bernard's son? But why pick on him?" Jonnet exclaimed.

"Oh, they had it agreed to their satisfaction – that, off work after his accident, he was short of money and hoped to get some that way. They even invited me to think so too – until I told them I had had it straight from his mother that, over and above his sick pay, Axel had paid him double wages since the accident happened. Berik Bernard indeed!

Working at The Broadlands since he was knee-high to a bee! As well suspect *Munt* of cutting up newspapers for the nasty purpose – or, for that matter, me or you. No, it is high time Axel stirred himself to find the real culprit, and I mean to tell him so *now*!"

As good as her word, she went to the telephone and related her story, following it with the tirade, "You have the evidence and you should act on it before we are all pointing the finger at one another and making more enemies of our friends than the nonsense is worth."

Whatever was Axel's reply, it came over only as a murmur of words to Jonnet, but Grethe snapped, "Give you time, you say? How much do you need, my friend? Meanwhile, I'd advise you to look nearer home than to honest men like Berik Bernard – What is it that you say? *You* did not accuse him? And what do I mean by 'nearer home'? oh no, *mijnheer*, I am no slander-monger like those others. I name no names. I leave it to you to prove me right or wrong in the notion I have of the affair." Then, suddenly abandoning the subject, she went on, "And the other piece of business between us? You are in the way of concluding that successfully, one hopes?"

That time Jonnet heard Axel's short laugh, though not his reply. But again Grethe played interpreter. "Not yet? I must be patient? Very well. I am more than content to leave it to you in the assurance that the outcome should be well worth our trouble," she concluded graciously. She replaced the receiver and turned to Jonnet.

"I think he will act, now that I have told him how we all suffer," she said. She did not explain what business in common it was that she and Axel had in hand.

But however Axel may or may not have "acted", the mystery was still unsolved by the time that Mervyn Hawke, his commission for Axel completed, was about to go back

153

to England. He and Jonnet discussed it on his last afternoon, on the way back from a leisurely tour of Overijssel,
the rich countryside bordering the vast expanse of the
Ijsselmeer.

In asking Mervyn whether Axel had been able to take the
matter any further, Jonnet told him of Grethe's telephoned
ultimatum, adding, "She told Axel she had her own ideas
about it, but not what they were, and she hasn't discussed
them with me."

Mervyn said, "Well, I suppose we all ask ourselves some
rather wild questions. For instance, the point that sticks
with me is that the anonymous letter said my design had
been loosely based on a Breughel winter scene. Yet the only
time I remember mentioning Breughel to anyone was in a
sort of aside to you on the evening after the opera, when
we discussed my plan. Of course Axel knew, and may have
passed it on to any of his workpeople. But he doesn't remember doing so, and if he did not —"

"If not, that could narrow it down to the people who
heard you that night," Jonnet finished for him thoughtfully.
"But that's impossible! There were only the six of us, and
it couldn't have been any of us, even though Axel declared
he meant to suspect everyone. And in proof that it couldn't
have been, you've forgotten that the writer wanted to be
paid for his information. Therefore it must have been
someone who expected to make something out of it. He
may have had a score against Axel too, but I should think
his chief motive was money."

Mervyn agreed, "Yes, that's true, and I've probably
overplayed the Breughel idea. Any of you who heard me
could have passed it on. But let's forget it, shall we? I'd
thought of stopping for tea here," and he pulled up at a
restaurant in the old town of Kampen.

Towards the end of the meal they had the oak-beamed

tea-room to themselves, so that there was no witness when he reached for Jonnet's hand and gently stroked the back of it with his thumb.

"Of all the times I have been over, staying with Axel, I've enjoyed this the most. Mainly because of meeting you, Jonnet. We've had fun, haven't we?" he asked.

She nodded. "A lot."

"I've got to get back and go on earning my living. But I'm going to miss you. And you me?"

"Yes," she said, meaning it.

"I'd hoped so. But I can see you again in England? When do you think of going back?"

"I don't quite know. I'd thought of staying six months with Tante Grethe, and that will be up soon. Or I might stay until the end of Dirk's school term. Then I must go back and pick up the threads of earning my living too."

"Well, it's a date we're going to keep as soon as you get back. You'll let me know when you mean to go? Promise? Or who knows, the way things seem to be shaping, I might be summoned back to Holland before then – as a guest at Axel's wedding."

"Oh – Yes." Jonnet hoped she had concealed her shock. "Is it imminent, then? Do you think he is –?"

– "Serious about Saskia? To be frank, I hope not. But you can't very well say to a chap, 'Look, man, you're wasting your talents,' when you're not in his confidence about the thing at all."

"And you're not? I could wish you were."

Mervyn's glance was swift and sharp. "You do? Why?"

(*Because even cruel certainty would be better than all this doubt.*) But unable to say that, Jonnet substituted, "Because I don't think Saskia is worthy of him either, and from his experience of her, Dirk knows she isn't. So that if Axel had confided in you, it might be because he valued

155

your advice, and he might have listened to you." (It wasn't the truth, but it had to serve.)

Mervyn agreed, "Possibly, though I doubt my right to dissuade him if he's made up his mind. For instance, I'd see the man further who tried to turn me against you."

Jonnet blushed. "It's not the same thing at all," she said.

"Isn't it?"

"We – don't know each other well enough."

"But if I can go on seeing you when you are in England, can't we improve on that?" He waited, but when she did not answer, he said quietly, "All right. I suppose I've known that it hasn't meant the same for you as for me, but I've hoped. And I may do that?"

She shook her head. "I don't think so, Mervyn. Not beyond our being friends. And that isn't fair to you."

"Could you allow me to decide that?" he asked dryly.

"I'm sorry –"

"Don't be. I'll settle for friendship. It's been good so far – a bonus I hadn't expected, and I don't want to lose it." He sat back, squaring his shoulders. "Meanwhile, in its name, will you make time to wish me Bon Voyage at Schiphol tomorrow?"

Grateful to him, Jonnet said, "I'd like to. How do I get there?"

"I'm giving up the car tonight and having a taxi. I'll send it out for you first, and after I've gone, the driver can bring you home," he told her.

But when she was expecting the taxi the next afternoon, instead it was Mervyn himself, driven by Axel, who came for her. He left the passenger seat to join her in the back, Axel explaining, "I don't know why this character thought he must go by taxi, when I was available as chauffeur."

At the airport Mervyn went through his flight formalities and they had tea in the restaurant. When he had to leave them at the door of the departure lounge, he took Jonnet's hand and after a moment's hesitation, drew her towards him and kissed her. Axel, standing by, said, "Don't mind me," with an air of giving his blessing to a relationship which he took for granted. And it seemed that he did when, in the car on the return journey, he said abruptly, "The man is in love with you. But I suppose you know that?"

Jonnet stared straight ahead. "He hasn't told me so," she said.

"Though he doesn't appear to mind telling the world. That's the second time I've seen him kiss you in public."

"It's only the second time ever."

He turned a wry glance upon her. "Oh, come!" he urged.

"And neither time meant a thing."

"Didn't say a thing to you, nor mean a thing from him? And if neither, what a waste! Now when I kiss a girl I always mean something by it. Though not always the same thing, nor even the same thing to the same girl."

Jonnet said stiffly, "That's rather too cryptic for me to follow, I'm afraid. But if you insist, this afternoon Mervyn was only saying Au Revoir until, as he hopes, we meet again in England."

"He could have put his fond farewell into words. couldn't he? He did to me. But when are you going back? I hear Dirk is taking a break and going over for Whitsun, but you mustn't go with him."

"I hadn't meant to."

"Wise girl, or you'd find yourself playing gooseberry."

Jonnet's head jerked round in surprise. "To him and Gertrud Spetz, do you mean? How did you know she was going to England too?"

"Dirk told me. But if he hadn't, I have my spies," Axel said loftily. "Anyway, Amsterdam lays on some slapstick

157

fun at Whitsun – mainly for the children – which you might like to see."

"Really? I've never been much taken with slapstick, I'm afraid."

"And particularly with Dutch slapstick? Tch, tch!" he clucked in disapproval, "there's your naughty prejudice at work again. What an uneasy death it's having, *if* it's dying at all, after all our trouble. But I shall stage a party for Whitsun, and you must come."

A party! – with Saskia preening herself as his favourite guest; perhaps even flaunting the plain gold ring which by Dutch tradition would show they were engaged. The very thought soured Jonnet's tongue as she replied, "Come? In what capacity, would you suggest? As – gooseberry, perhaps?"

There was a pause. Then to her discomfiture he laughed aloud. "You make your point," he said. "But no, on second thoughts we won't *have* a party. For old-time battle's sake, we'll make it a twosome – for just you and me. Consider it a date, and I'll call for you myself."

CHAPTER NINE

I NEEDN'T go, Jonnet told herself after her silence must have allowed Axel to assume she had accepted his fiat of an invitation.

I can stage a seizure of – well, of something dire. Or Tante Grethe must want me to finish some urgent work for her. No, that won't do, for he's quite capable of ringing up and finding it wasn't true. Well then, I must – yes, I must have promised Dirk to meet and entertain some friends of his, over in Holland for Whitsun. But not in Amsterdam. Say at Arnhem or Valkenburg, anywhere as far-flung as possible, and they can be about to cross the border into Germany, so that I shan't have to account for them later.

For I will *not* be sandwiched between one of his dates with Saskia and the next! He'll have had to tell her he's invited me alone, and if I have to meet her between now and then, I can just hear her forgiving me ever so sweetly for stealing him from her for just one day. *No!*

And yet – the pull of her need to be with him, just with him and no one else, if only for battle's sake, had kept "No, thank you" from her lips on the drive from the airport, and still kept her from writing or telephoning her excuses during the days which followed. There was time enough before Whitsun yet; if necessary, Dirk's mythical friends could arrive and need her company at the eleventh hour. And while her head and her pride hadn't yet said a definite No, perhaps she could indulge her heart in wishing and hoping for the outside chance which would allow her to say Yes.

Meanwhile Munt had honoured his promise to find time

to explain to her his method of dealing with his freak daffodil, botanically a narcissus, as he curtly pointed out.

He demonstrated how the narcissus bulb fragmented into two or three smaller bulbs; how the tulip behaved differently by producing each season usually one flowering sized bulb, carrying a cluster of tiny bulblets at its base. The junior bulbs of the narcissus were capable of flowering the next season; the bulblets of the tulip must be "grown on" up to flowering size. He had records of his Boss of Gold having maintained its freakhood since the young bulbs' first season of flowering, but the growth cycle of Jonnet's Murillo tulip was going to call for much more patience. However, when the field bulbs were lifted in June she should see how he would separate and preserve the bulblets for replanting.

"June? I may be going back to England by then," she told him.

He showed a dour interest in the news. "And I suppose you expect the crop to ready itself for lifting before time, just to suit you?" he demanded.

She dismissed the absurdity. "No, of course not. I'll stay to see the lifting of this one, but I shan't be here much longer after that."

"You go then – but you come back?"

"Probably not. Not this year, at any rate."

He put his question another way. "You do not stay to live here? Why not? Because you see now that Mejuffrouw Handel means to hold on to her own, and that you gain nothing by waiting to occupy her shoes?"

To think she had flattered herself he had softened towards her! As evenly as she could, Jonnet said, "I'd hoped you'd know by now that I came here just on a visit, neither hoping nor waiting for anything at all. And my aunt has known all along that I have to go back."

He shook his head. "But no, you are wrong there. She thinks that you stay."

"She may have done at first, but I'm sure she doesn't now."

"Ah, but she means that you stay. She has told me so, and that she has hung out a broom for you." He paused, his old eyes narrowing. "But these words you tell me you do not understand?"

Jonnet flushed. "I do now. Said of a girl, they mean that she is in need of a husband. I'm not, so you are mistaken in thinking that Tante Grethe has one in view for me."

"Then why did she tell me she had?"

"I don't believe she ever did. But if you claim she did mention some man to you, who was it?"

"The *mijnheer* next door." He jerked a head in the direction of The Broadlands. "Mijnheer Axel Keyser. And how are you to know whether or not the Murillo holds its colour, if you are not here to watch it through the seasons?"

"I shan't be here. I realise I shan't know what happens to it."

"Then why have I wasted good time on you or on it?" he demanded, and then unexpectedly achieved an expression as near to a smile as she supposed his rusty features could manage at short notice. "I think you should stay, *mejuffrouw*," he said.

She shook her head. "I – can't," she said wretchedly, and went in search of Grethe, to question the truth of Munt's story of her matchmaking.

Accused, Grethe remained unmoved. "But if you remember, niece, I told you of my hopes that you would marry one of our countrymen?" she parried.

"Yes. Within an hour or two of my arrival, which I thought ridiculous," Jonnet complained.

"And I suppose you knew I thought well of an affair

161

between you and Axel Keyser. If you remember also, I doubted very much whether he would spend so much time with you, merely to quarrel with you. This is not the way men behave."

"It's the way *he* behaved. Mostly," Jonnet added as a sop to the rare sweet times when he had been kind, and when they had agreed, and when they had laughed together.

Grethe ignored the qualifying "mostly", and persisted, "Then if it was so, you must have provoked him. As, it would seem, you did. For you lost him to Saskia Moet, did you not? And about that I remember telling you at the time that, though it was then too late, you need not have allowed the matter to have happened as it did."

Jonnet agreed dully, "I remember too, though as Axel never had that kind of interest in me, I can hardly be said to have 'lost' him to Saskia, can I?"

"True enough," Grethe conceded. "And as you would not be as annoyed as you are with me for my plans, had you wanted to keep him for yourself, there will have been, as they say, no cream spilt."

Jonnet persisted, "I still don't want you to have the wrong idea about my friendship with Axel."

"Of course not, of course not," Grethe soothed. "And perhaps I should have known I was wrong when he allowed you to become so intimate with his friend, the Englishman." She paused and scrutinised the state of her inevitable knitting, then added briskly, "And what is it one hears of Dirk? That he has so far recovered from Saskia's betrayal of him that he is now happily courting another girl? Is that so?"

"Yes. Gertrud Spetz."

"Ah, a girl of good Dutch stock. Her father is pastor to one of the city parish churches."

162

"Yes, I know. But how did you hear about her and Dirk?"

"From Axel, who is naturally pleased."

"Don't you mean his conscience is relieved?"

Grethe drew down her spectacles and eyed Jonnet over them. "His conscience? What has conscience to do with it?"

Jonnet said tartly, "A lot, I'd have thought, from the unscrupulous way he took Saskia away from Dirk."

"But you and I agreed she was not the right girl for Dirk. Therefore we should applaud Axel, shouldn't we? Besides, he could not have enticed Saskia away, if she were not willing to go."

"Well, it was to be expected she would go, once Axel chose to turn his charm on her. How could Dirk compete with that?"

As soon as she had spoken, Jonnet saw the trap she had laid for herself and qualified hastily, "For I suppose Axel has charm – for anyone who is susceptible to it."

"Which you congratulate yourself you are not, *h'm*?" Grethe asked smoothly, resuming her knitting.

Hoping to enforce her earlier point, Jonnet said, "It's not so difficult to be proof against the charm of a man who provokes you into arguing against him most of the time."

"And yet, as I have said before, what a *very* great deal of his time Axel would appear to have spent in ruffling you, before he took to courting Saskia instead!" Grethe retorted with a confident air of having annexed the last word.

Jonnet let her have it. But that settled the question of Whitsun. Now she could *not* admit that she proposed to spend a whole day in Axel's company by choice! Of course she had never seriously considered doing so . . . Or had she? Whatever the answer was to that, she was guiltily glad that, with Whitsun still a week or two away, she hadn't to cast any ideas or burn any boats of decision just yet.

Now the fields were turning mostly brown again, as the dying foliage of the spent flowers crisped and flattened, though here and there, there was compensation in the promise of the summer lilies and of the Dutch iris which would dress itself overall in blues and golds and whites, come June.

Jonnet told herself she would wait to see the main crop of the tulips lifted; she wanted to be there to see Munt's first care for "her" Murillo, even if she would not see his last. But then she would go, before the money she had allowed herself for her stay had run out, and before it became more difficult *to* go.

It was Mevrouw Bernard, calling to borrow a knitting pattern from Grethe, who brought the news that all the Broadlands workers had been cleared of having sent the anonymous letter, as Axel had let it be known that he had proof now of who had been guilty of it, and it was not one of them.

"That's good. But it needed me to call him to his duty about it, to protect honest names from the gossips' tongues," Grethe claimed.

"My Berik's name among them, had you heard?" the old lady asked.

"I had indeed. But if it wasn't any of the wickedly bandied names, who was it, then?"

But that Mevrouw Bernard did not know. The message had come through Axel's secretary who, if she were to be believed, knew nothing either – only that Axel had declared the matter now to be closed.

"The tiresome man!" Grethe grumbled. "While he accuses no one, does he not realise there will still be rumour? And now, of all those who could have done it, who remains? Who but we others, his neighbours? While his silence protects someone, we still suffer. I declare, if he does nothing more about it, I shall tell him roundly that he has no right to –! Mevrouw Bernard, you will take *koffietafel* with Jonnet and me before you go?"

But whether or not Grethe spoke her mind to Axel later, she did not confide to Jonnet. Jonnet suspected she may have done, but getting no satisfaction from him, would not admit it. For to the stalwart Grethe, Jonnet realised by now, a battle lost to anyone but Munt was a matter for shame.

And then, without previous warning even to her sister, Letti was to drop her bombshell of surprise. She made another unaccustomed visit to the farm to do it, annoyed to find, when she called, that Grethe had gone to Amsterdam with Munt, but so full of her news that she announced it to Jonnet instead.

"I am giving up my house at the end of the month and taking Saskia to Paris," she said.

"Taking Saskia *away*? Just now?" Jonnet's jaw had dropped. "Tante Letti, this is a surprise! I thought –"

"You need not tell me. I know very well what you thought," her aunt cut in. "I thought it myself – and happily. But not any more, and as the last thing I want is to see my darling girl the mere toy of a philanderer like Axel Keyser, what could I do but encourage her decision to throw *him* over before *he* has a chance to cast her aside like – like a worn-out glove?"

Later Jonnet was to realise that her sudden impulse to laugh sprang from something other – a sense of reprieve? of new ease of mind? – than her amusement at Letti's resort to timeworn clichés. Next, she will accuse Axel of wasting the best years of Saskia's life, she thought, then said aloud,

"You mean Saskia has broken with Axel, and that's why you are taking her away? But you were so pleased about it, Tante Letti! You told me at the Corso that you thought i an excellent match for her, didn't you?"

"And so I did, and was as ready as any mother to allow him time to declare his intentions. But now it seems he has none – after monopolising her and keeping every other eligible man at bay! – and she sees that he only wants her for the plaything he has made of all his other conquests, though naturally she is quite *heartbroken*, she has sent him away."

What could Jonnet say? That she was sorry when, sceptical of the intensity of Saskia's heartbreak, she wasn't at all? At last she managed, "I think you shouldn't be too unhappy about it, Tante Letti. If Axel can't make up his mind about Saskia, perhaps it's as well that they should break up before it's too late. After all, Dirk was courting her before Axel did, and she is so – so attractive to men that I'm sure she will soon meet another one who will help her to forget Axel quite soon. Especially if, as you say, you mean to take her away to fresh scenes and among new people. That should help."

Letti dabbed her eyes dry of a tear or two (of pity for her own role or of compassion for Saskia? – Jonnet wondered which.) "Oh, that I shall certainly do," she claimed, adding, with an air of setting the record straight, "And you mustn't think that Dirk was by any means the first man in my little girl's life. Why, ever since she left school they have been falling for her – everywhere she goes!"

Jonnet nodded gravely. "I can imagine," she said.

"And I expect we may make a permanency of Paris," Letti went on. "Or if not, perhaps the Riviera or even Rome. There is nothing to hold me here in Holland, and Dutchmen on the whole are all so *dull*." She rose, her mission complete. As Jonnet showed her to the door she said, "Very awkward that Grethe should be out. But you can tell her that I called and what I have decided, and both of you must come to luncheon with us one day before we leave," – an occasion on which Jonnet determined she would have the most pressing of previous engagements. Tante Letti on the defensive for her ewe lamb was quite enough. Saskia playing that same cruelly deceived and wounded lamb would be too much.

Grethe's reaction to the news was odd, her calm comment of "So soon?" reminding Jonnet forcibly of the lack of surprise with which she had first heard of Saskia's jilting of Dirk in favour of Axel. It struck Jonnet that now, as then, she might almost have been awaiting it as a foregone conclusion – which was surely impossible, considering how few illusions she had of Saskia's tenacity in pursuit of her own advantage? Grethe *must* have expected Saskia to hold on to Axel, however dilatory he was about proposing marriage! And yet her "So soon?" had sounded as if only the timing of the break-up had taken her unawares.

Puzzled, Jonnet questioned, "You don't seem very surprised, Tante Grethe? Do you mean you thought this might happen?"

"Some time, yes. I'd have expected it to take rather longer, that is all."

"But why weren't you surprised?"

"Why? Because Axel is no fool, and he has known Saskia for quite long enough to know her for a minx with no heart and less brain and a chocolate-box prettiness that won't last beyond her twenties. Oh yes, I could have told you pretty certainly that to him she was only one more in the queue of girls he has kissed and left in his time!"

"Among whom – also in the queue – you think I have been too?" Jonnet queried, hurt.

Grethe nodded. "You too, niece. You had your chance with him, and might have been the one to keep him, had you wanted to, if you had ever allowed him time to kiss you between all your quarrels about this and that."

"I'm glad you said 'had I wanted to'," Jonnet rejoined.

"But of course." Grethe's tone held bland agreement. "Haven't you told me often enough of your wordy fisti-cuffs, and that you found Axel nothing but a scold? How-ever – no, I never did expect him to take this latest affair as far as marriage – only that he would not have brought it to an end quite yet."

"Though had he any option? After all, it was Saskia who got impatient, waiting, and broke it off with *him*," Jonnet reminded her.

Grethe's bright eyes blinked, then stared. "And you be-lieve poor Letti's story that this was the way it was?"

"That's what she said."

"And wouldn't any mother, or stepmother for that mat-ter – as even I, an old spinster, know? Oh no, child, you can depend upon it that it was not Saskia who broke it off. She would be far too aware of his value as a prize. But you must see that Letti's devotion to her could not allow anyone to think she was jilted. That is why she is whisking the girl away before there is talk. And of course, to save Letti's face, I shall pretend to believe her. As you must too. Axel can take care of himself. His back is broad and he can outstare the pointed fingers well enough – especially if, presently, he is 'on with the new', as they say."

Jonnet winced. "I don't think how you can be so sure that Tante Letti was only shielding Saskia's pride about all this," she said.

"Ah," replied Grethe darkly.

"What do you mean –'Ah'?"

"Simply that I don't expect you, young as you are, to understand the experience which tells me it is so, even though Letti must not guess that I know it is. And now, will you go and ask Munt about the invoice for the latest load of fertilizer from Meyerbeers – whether he used it as a towel for his hands, or what became of it, if not? To that man a bill or a cheque or a final demand could be so much blank paper, for all he bothers about it! And don't let him keep you gossiping about freak bulbs he has known in his time. Come straight back," Grethe ordered, in an abrupt switch from personal issues to business.

Jonnet went, her relation with Munt now so well founded that she could even report to him with impunity Grethe's suspicions as to his use of the missing invoice. He denied it. The paper in question was discovered, clamped down by a flower-pot; she smoothed out its wrinkles and returned with it to the office, while another part of her mind was churning away at a question which she wanted to answer with Yes, though not knowing how she could.

Since Tante Letti's news, the case had altered, she argued in favour. Now – just supposing – she allowed Axel to take her to Amsterdam at Whitsun, it would no longer be a date snatched from Saskia's claim on his company; it wouldn't be the sandwich which her pride scorned. What was more, it would make unnecessary the lie about her urgent summons to Arnhem or wherever. And yet more – she wanted to go with him quite badly. But against, there was the daunting thought of admitting her acceptance to Grethe, who would put on a "The lady doth protest too much" look and could hardly be expected to believe in Axel's provocation of her, ever again. Besides, she was only too aware of the rank folly of falling again under his spell, after determining to wrest free. (Just once, could it matter? the pro argument pleaded. But you know it could, the con side ruled.)

In the end she chose the easy way and did nothing, as hitherto. After all, the Arnhem bit would appear all the more urgent if she postponed announcing it until almost the eve of the holiday. While she hadn't said No, there was still a chance she could say Yes – And then, through no decision nor irresolution of her own, at the last moment the matter was solved for her – at least as far as confession to her aunt was concerned.

When she had taken Axel's telephone call she was able to tell Grethe, "Axel Keyser just rang up to say that as her father is still in plaster and can't cycle, he is taking Lysbet Bernard to Amsterdam tomorrow and he has asked me to go with them. He will collect Lysbet first and then come for me."

Grethe nodded. "Ah yes, the Lazybones revels – the once-a-year piece of mischief the children are allowed. Is he taking you by car?"

"No. It seems Lysbet wants to cycle, as all her school friends will be on theirs, so he suggests we all do."

"And you are willing?"

"To cycle? Oh yes, if that's what Lysbet wants."

"I meant," Grethe corrected, "that I am surprised that you can bring yourself to accept any more invitations from Axel, considering how he irks you."

Jonnet felt her colour rise. "Yes, well – I think he wants me to help him to keep an eye on Lysbet," she hedged, deeming it unnecessary to mention that Axel's original invitation had been for a tête-à-tête, or that, but for the saving grace of Lysbet's company, she would still have been torn between inclinations which she knew to be rash and a lying ruse which she would have despised.

She had heard that the Whitsun revels were a cross between a bunfeast, a fair and a Bonfire Night, but when Axel and Lysbet arrived for her, she was quite unprepared for the medley of strange luggage which bulged from Lysbet's saddlebag, and dangled from both her own handlebars and from Axel's, acting as reserve transport.

There were a bent poker, two or three bottomless sauce-

170

pans, some odd shoes, a broken alarm clock, chipped jam-jars, some worn-down brushes and as many other domestic throw-outs as the child had been able to amass and to per-suade Axel to help to carry.

Lysbet giggled at Jonnet's stare of wonder. "For the Lazybones knocking. We all bring some rubbish for it," she explained, eyeing Jonnet's handlebars, bare of any burden. "If I'd thought you could have carried some, I'd have brought more."

"Roping in another packhorse," Axel intervened. "You've got quite enough junk as it is, young Lysbet. And once you start in on this knocking racket, Jonnet and I are going to pretend we don't know you. Understood?"

Lysbet giggled again and in answer to Jonnet's question as they set out, described how the children went round the streets, knocking on doors where, should they not be opened at once, they fastened assorted rubbish to the knockers and with a shout of "Lazybones! Lazybones!" ran away.

"Metal stuff is best, because it makes a lovely 'clank' when the people do open the door," she explained. "I had ready some very old flatirons too —"

"With which I refused to be loaded," put in Axel.

Jonnet laughed. "I should think you make yourselves very popular with the householders. But how do you know they do come to the door, if you have run away?"

"Oh, they nearly always come. They expect us today, you see. And we don't go far. We hide and watch what happens."

"And if the people are out, or are unsporting enough not to answer the door, then the little monsters go back and retrieve the rubbish to use for some other victim," said Axel. "Then later on in the day a lot of it finds its way into the canals, when they throw in Old Devil Winter. You'll see."

It was a bright sunny day, and in the city the streets and bridges wore an air of holiday, with children afoot and on bicycles milling everywhere, and for once, the cars giving way to them. The canals were full of craft, their passengers waiting to watch from the water the drowning of the traditional straw effigies which would mark the passing of that year's winter. The main centres of interest were the many bakers' and pastrycooks' shops, where crowds of children had gathered, expectant of something to happen.

When it did, it took the unusual form of the sounding of a horn, followed by the emergence of a chef in costume bearing a pastrycook's wooden tray on his head – the signal that the Whitsun dough-balls, to be eaten hot with butter and doused with treacle, were ready for consumption. At sight of the chef, the crowds surged in to buy and eat their fill before, fortified and sticky, they were ready for whatever diversions the rest of the day had to offer.

Lysbet had gone to join her cronies, after making a time for a later meeting with Axel and Jonnet, who pedalled slowly round the residential streets, watching the bands of knockers at their mischievous work which, to give them credit, the householders seemed to take in good part, making a playfully shaken fist their only threat to the nuisance. Even, sometimes, the miscreants were sought out and given money or invited in. "Like the carol-singers at home at Christmas," Jonnet commented, and then as a thought occurred to her, asked Axel,

"Used you to do this too, when you were a child?"

He nodded. "Making Old Devil Winters, dough-balls, lazybones knocking – the lot. What is comparable in England?"

"Well, hot cross buns at Easter, and pennies for the guy on the Fifth of November, I suppose." As Jonnet had put her question she had had a sudden longing to have known

172

what Axel had been like as a small boy, as a teenager, and at the same age as she was now. For that was an essential part of loving – wanting depth and background behind the person you loved; wanting to share your own with them. Everyone had family jokes and stories to tell against themselves, and she would like to hear Axel's; to tell him hers.

Before they were due to meet Lysbet they lingered for a while on one of the squares where there was a roundabout, and stalls selling balloons and chocolate-filled clogs and miniature windmills and Winter Devils. Axel bought one of these latter for Jonnet, saying, "Next Whitsun, you and Mervyn Hawke can throw it into the Serpentine or the Thames or whatever water is handiest, and remember us."

"It wouldn't mean anything there. I'd rather throw it into a canal here. Besides," she added, not without a touch of malice, "in England we reckon to kill off our winter long before Whitsun."

"Really? Well, pardon *me*," Axel retorted with elaborate courtesy, "but I *have* been in England in mid-April and seen icicles a foot long on the house-eaves; not to mention hailstones the size of marbles doing their stuff in May."

Jonnet laughed and gave in. "I only said we 'reckon' to have finished with winter," she reminded him.

When they parked their bicycles and went for coffee and cakes at a pavement table she wondered whether he would apologise for turning their date into a threesome with Lysbet. But as with their promised visit to the Concertgebouw, of which he had made a party of six instead, he made no excuses for bringing Lysbet. Almost as if he sensed that, without Lysbet, she might have been in two minds about coming with him, she was thinking when he surprised her by asking suddenly,

"Supposing my affair with Saskia hadn't come to the sticky end of which I'm sure you must have heard, would you have kept this date with me today?" And then, at her glance of embarrassment, "All right — one doesn't have to be clairvoyant to guess that, without Lysbet as a go-between, you wouldn't have come. Am I right?"

She looked away from his scrutiny. "I might not," she admitted.

"Too proud to play second fiddle to Saskia? Why should you have been, when I'm just as guilty of cutting in on Hawke?"

"It's not at all the same thing. Saskia and you were never just the good friends that Mervyn and I were — are still."

"And how right you are, at that," Axel agreed. "Saskia's type doesn't look for friendship with a man; it has to be the amorous bit or nothing."

"Which, until it didn't amuse you any longer, you seem to have offered her quite successfully."

If Jonnet expected him to be abashed, she was disappointed. "Oh, do you think we made rather a beautiful couple? I'm so glad," he said genially. "What a pity, wasn't it, that it couldn't last? But there, that's life," he added with a mock sigh.

"Are you saying then that you never meant it should last? That to you it was just — another affair with a girl?"

"Not just another affair this time. Not this one. This was designed to serve a purpose — and did."

"I see. The purpose being to show that you could take Saskia away from Dirk just when you wanted to? Yes, I know I've accused you of this before and though you wouldn't admit it then, you do now?"

He nodded. "Guilty. I do now."

Jonnet gathered the tattered threads of her patience. "I wonder you *dare*!" she exclaimed. "Of — of all the despicable motives —!"

"But though successful, not the only one."

"Yes, so I remember you said before."

"You don't want to hear what it was?"

"Not particularly," she lied. "And I only hope Saskia doesn't regret having wasted her time with you, believing you were serious, when you weren't."

"Sorry for Saskia? Don't be," he advised. "She was born a scalp-collector. She won't be losing any sleep over me."

"I'm glad you can salve your conscience so." Jonnet stood up. "However, I don't think I want to hear any more about an amorous intrigue which doesn't seem to have had much real heart to it on either side. If you don't mind, I'm going home."

He stood too and loosely but firmly shackled her wrist with his fingers. "You are doing nothing of the kind," he stated. "In a few minutes now we're keeping our rendezvous with Lysbet – remember?"

"You can keep it."

"And explain to the child that you've taken yourself off in a silly huff?"

"You don't have to put it like that –"

"I shall, if you don't stay. You didn't have to come, but I'm not letting you spoil Lysbet's day with us. Besides, if you back out now, hours before you are expected, what are you going to tell Grethe?"

"I needn't tell her anything."

"And can you see her letting you get away with that? No, my girl –" he released her wrist and looked at his watch – "even if you have to suffer the rest of the day wearing a fixed *Pagliacci* grin on your face, you're going to see it through."

CHAPTER TEN

Jonnet saw it through.

It helped to have Lysbet as a kind of buffer state between Axel and herself, and indeed, presently she wondered whether, this time, she had allowed him to goad her too easily.

After all, he had only confirmed what he had allowed her to guess already about his deliberate enticement of Saskia. And as Grethe had remarked, Saskia's defection had done Dirk nothing but good. Axel's assumption of an affair between her and Mervyn Hawke wasn't new either, so she could have passed over both without comment and in reasonable dignity. Instead, she had flogged herself into that petty show of temper with which he had dealt so summarily, and of which she was now ashamed.

If she hadn't refused to listen, he might have confided to her whatever other reasons he had had for entangling with Saskia, and the curiosity which she had denied to him, admitted to wanting to know what they were; wanting to hope they were less self-centred and arrogant than the one which had prompted his shameless *coup* against Dirk. But it was too late now. After today's showdown, he wasn't likely to invite her anywhere again. She would be left to her jealousy and her regrets, and he would be free to work the magic of his charm on the next girl in the queue ...

With Lysbet – who claimed a highly successful Lazybones knocking – they toured the streets slowly, went for a trip through the canals, watched the ceremonial drowning of the Devils and had a luscious meal of roast duckling and asparagus while watching a display of fireworks from the balcony of the waterside restaurant they chose.

As it was a children's frolic, it was not very late when, most of the fun being over, Lysbet agreed she was willing to go home. By then the streets were filled with cars and cyclists, all on the same errand, the latter weaving their way between the cars in single file of no more than two abreast, in accordance with the city's law. Jonnet rode ahead with Lysbet on her near side. Axel followed, his partner frequently changing as tempting gaps in the traffic opened up.

Except for these latter intrepids no one was speeding, but as the procession was passing a line of parked cars, one of their doors was rashly flung open, to catch Lysbet's handlebars, causing her to swerve wildly in her effort to keep her balance. She failed. Before she fell, her bicycle struck Jonnet's back wheel from under her. Jonnet fell too – into the path of the latest speedster, who, however, managing to avoid her, shot away and disappeared, leaving behind him outraged cries and the screech of brakes as a following car rocked to a halt, only just short of the outstretched hand she had put up blindly in an effort to ward off the threat of its front wheels to her own body and to Lysbet's, just off from hers, beneath the pile of metal which was, or had been, their bicycles.

There was shouting, the crowd closing in, the dazzle of the car's headlights in her eyes, and then Axel was beside them both, kneeling after letting his own cycle drop, murmuring urgently, "Jonnet!" and *"Mijn lieveling!"* – the endearment meant for Lysbet, of course, since she hadn't enough English to understand "My darling."

Ready hands joined his in helping them to stand, and tongues clucked sympathy and anger as they recovered themselves shakily, both more shocked than hurt.

At sight of her twisted bicycle Lysbet began to cry and as Axel put an arm round her and drew her to him, over

177

her head he remarked grimly to Jonnet, "This is rather where we came in –" reminding her of the winter night of their second meeting, when Lysbet and her bicycle had been even less fortunate than now. He soothed the child, "Never mind, little one. It has probably only got a buckled wheel and broken lamps. If it's more than that, we'll see about a new one for you."

Then the police were there, asking questions, listening to witnesses, taking names and addresses, and taking measurements which proved that the overtaking car had pulled up in a laudably short distance. They dealt shortly and severely with the original culprit, who stood by the open door of his car, explaining that, as an English tourist, used to the English rule of the road, he had momentarily forgotten that he would be opening his door in the face of the overtaking traffic. Axel put Jonnet and Lysbet and their bicycles in the charge of the police while he went to fetch his car from the Herengracht, and a young policewoman took them to a nearby café to await his return.

At the cafe they washed and surveyed the damage to their clothes – for Jonnet, badly laddered tights and a torn hem and shirt; for Lysbet, begrimed knee-socks and shorts and a long tear in a sleeve. The policewoman gave first aid to Jonnet's cut wrist and Lysbet's grazed knees, warning them to attend at the hospital for anti-tetanus injections the next day. They had time for a cup of coffee, and then Axel came back to collect them and drive them home.

He took Lysbet in the front seat beside him, advising Jonnet to relax, if she could, in the back. She was only too glad to be left to try. Aching all over, even where she wasn't hurt, she wondered whether that was her delayed reaction to shock, whereas with Lysbet it was possibly taking the form of a continuous, excited stream of chatter which wasn't like her at all. Jonnet left Axel to respond to it, and

178

lay back, closing her eyes. What an end to a day which had begun so gaily for them all! she thought wearily – and surprised herself by coming to with a jerk as Axel pulled up at the Bernards' cottage.

She thrust back her hair. "I believe I've been asleep," she said.

"You have," he confirmed. "Lysbet spotted you in the driving mirror." And as she made to get out, "No. Stay where you are. I'll go in and explain what has happened, and then I'll take you on."

When he returned some time later to report that Lysbet, put to bed at once with hot chocolate as a nightcap, had already been asleep before he left, he didn't ask Jonnet into the front seat, but talked to her over his shoulder.

He asked conversationally, "Have you wondered why I dug in my heels and wouldn't let you leave when you put on that indignation act this afternoon?"

"You told me why. You said you wouldn't allow me to spoil Lysbet's day," she reminded him.

"Exactly. Putting the onus on Lysbet, because, while you were as mad as all that, I wasn't admitting to plans of my own which I didn't mean to have spoilt."

"Plans? What kind of plans?"

"For this evening, and not including Lysbet, whom I'd have taken home by car first. In short, dinner for two at home, prepared and served by Marthe, my daily woman – even chaperonage laid on, you see!"

"You – wanted me to have dinner with you tonight?"

"I *meant* you to have dinner with me tonight, if all this hadn't happened. But don't worry, I've called it off. When I went back for the car I sent Marthe away, because I knew you would want me to take you straight home."

"I'm – sorry. Perhaps another time," Jonnet murmured conventionally.

His glance met hers briefly in the driving mirror. "Does that mean you would have come without my having to hijack you? Or was 'another time' politeness for 'never'?"

"Neither. I meant I was sorry I lost my temper this afternoon, and if you had asked me to dine with you, I'd have liked to come."

"Really? I'm encouraged. Though whence the change of heart? Curiosity perhaps? Asking yourself whether or not you heard me calling you 'my darling' in the stress of the moment, back there in the city?"

Jonnet's face flamed. "Of course I heard you. But you said it to Lysbet – in Dutch."

"But I thought you understood Dutch?" They had reached the gates of The Broadlands on the way to the farm, and Axel drew up. "Encouraged to hear that you might have dined with me, may I suggest that if you feel equal to it, you'll accept a cup of coffee before I take you home?" he asked, and as she hesitated, "No caviare, I'm afraid. No roast swan. No *crêpes suzettes* or *bombe surprise*. Not even a cube of humble Gouda. No chaperon either. But will you come?"

Jonnet went, not daring to question why she did; only knowing that once again his magic had drawn her; that she had to make his will hers. Of course, for all his hints, he couldn't have meant to call her his darling. But she could hope, couldn't she, until they laughed it off, as they would have to?

Rash. Reckless. Wanton. How many words were there for the folly of actually inviting pain? For the moment she couldn't care, while *mijn lieveling* echoed in her ears. Or was that just another effect of shock?

As he helped her out of the car she flicked at the tear in her shirt. "I'm not exactly company-dressed for caviare or roast swan," she said. To which he replied mock-gallantly,

"If you hadn't mentioned it, I should never have noticed," and kept his arm lightly across her shoulders until he unlocked the door to the dark office and led the way through to his inner room.

He put her into one of the leather armchairs and busied himself making the coffee. He went to the drinks cabinet. "A liqueur with it? I can offer you one of several."

"No, thank you." She was lightheaded enough already! He brought the coffee and sat down near her. "One thing," he remarked easily, "Grethe won't be worrying that you are not yet back."

"Oh – did she know then that you were going to ask me to dinner?"

"And that I might keep you late. In fact, she advised it, mentioning that in her opinion it was high time."

Jonnet's cup shook slightly in its saucer. "High time that you asked me to dine with you? What did she mean?"

"More, I think, that she considered it to be time the joint scheme on which she and I have been engaged began to show results."

"A business scheme of Tante Grethe's and yours?" Jonnet had recalled their talk on the telephone. "But what could that have to do with me, with dinner tonight, with – anything?"

He looked amused at her bewilderment. "Not a business scheme. More of an intrigue. And I don't excuse the word, for you used it yourself today of the Saskia interlude, and that is exactly what it was." He laughed. "You've never seen Grethe as a mistress of conspiracy, have you? Not that I'm so bad at plot and counterplot myself. In fact, I was the prime mover in the idea, whereas she suggested certain likely side-effects which, if they happened, were entirely agreeable to me."

Jonnet put aside her coffee. "I don't know what you are

181

talking about. You'll have to explain."

"And if I do, you won't walk out on me, bent on trudging your own way home? You'll still be here when I finish?"

She bit her lip. "I'll try to be."

"Well then, perhaps I wasn't the prime mover. You were."

"*I?*"

"When you wanted to insist on your right to bludgeon Dirk with advice against Saskia. When I knew in my bones that that wasn't the way to do it, and that I had a pretty shrewd idea of what was."

"What was what?"

"The only way to convince Dirk just what a little weathervane he was courting in Saskia. In short, by demonstration and example; the finesse which you scorned. Which was where I flattered myself I came in – by drawing her fire for as long as it might take Dirk to come to his senses, knowing that she hadn't any heart either for him or for me, and that when the time came for our showdown, nothing but her pride was going to suffer. That – and her jealousy of you. And it worked, didn't it? Dirk was cured, more or less painlessly, and still without a clue as to why he should be grateful to me."

Jonnet stared straight in front of her, trying to piece all that together, to glean from it some meaning which she could understand. At last she said slowly,

"Yes, Dirk was cured, though not as painlessly as you think. You don't kill love as easily as all that. And I remember, when I asked you, you said that your affair with Saskia wasn't resolved yet. So you are telling me now that you never meant it to be – that it was all laid on for Dirk's sake – to show him what a turncoat Saskia was?"

"*Mostly* for Dirk's good," Axel amended. "There were other issues at stake."

"But – Saskia?" Jonnet doubted. "Had you the right to –?"

"With no other girl I've ever met – no right at all," he agreed, his eyes grave. "But knowing Saskia for what she was, and is still, for I doubt if she has learned her lesson – yes, I think one had the right. And realising she was a cheat and a traitor too made the final scene a bit easier to stage."

"A – cheat?" Jonnet murmured.

He nodded. "The anonymous letter to Het Bloemkwekery. That was her doing. You hadn't guessed?"

"*Saskia*? Of course not. It must have been someone who wanted money for it. The letter said so, didn't it?"

"A very nice touch of double bluff, that. As Grethe suspected and suggested to me, though naming no names, she claimed. And then Hawke did his bit by worrying aloud that he hadn't mentioned beyond my party – after *Fledermaus*, just the six of us, remember? – that his design had been inspired by Breughel."

"Yes, he told me as much," Jonnet said.

"And for me it dropped everything into place. It *had* to be Saskia. Her mention of Breughel in the letter fairly proved it. Besides, she had cause. To someone of her make-up, every presentable female is a potential rival, and when her particular radar system bleeped that you had more than potential, that as far as I was concerned, you were a dangerous fact, she saw the letter as a way of getting even with both of us. I must confess I'd have liked to see her, snipping away at all those newspapers! Her main mistake, of course, was her belief that she had to go to the very top, to Het Bloemkwekery, my biggest competitor. But she wasn't mistaken in thinking she had to be jealous of you. And not just as the ice queen either."

"She thought that you –? Oh no, that's impossible!"

He drew his chair closer and sat on the edge of it. They

were knee to knee, and he took both her hands in his.

"Only to your ramrod way of thinking, my darling," he said. "Never to mine – from the very first time you stood up to me, did your best to cut me down to size, to pulverise me with argument and dust down your hands, thinking you had succeeded–"

"I never did," Jonnet said shakily.

"Exactly. But neither did I, and that was where the fun came in. I said to myself, 'Here's my girl at last – with all the spirit and rebound of a ball; all the others, dead shuttlecocks by comparison. Speaks her mind, has a wicked will of her own, would go to the stake in loyalty to Dirk. Walks like a young queen, smiles with the whole of her face, enthuses like a teenager and contrives to be the one girl I shall enjoy kissing ten, twenty, thirty years hence – yes, indeed, here's my girl!' "

"Though you've enjoyed kissing a good many others. You've said so," Jonnet reminded him.

"Of course," he retorted, the blue eyes innocently wide. "How do you think connoisseurs are made? They're not born that way, recognising the best. They arrive at it by trial and error, and I – well, I'm there now, at experiment's journey's end. Do you believe me, sweetheart? Can you? More important still – do you want to?"

She looked down at her hands, enfolded in his. "I've wanted to – for a very long time," she said.

He thrust aside his chair and knelt, his arms about her body. "Since when?" he urged.

"I think – it was one day when Mevrouw Bernard reminded me that you can be hurt more by being misunderstood or misjudged by someone you love than by anyone else. She seemed to guess that I would rather fight with you than be flattered to the eyebrows by another man. She called herself an 'old one' and told me that one day I should re-

184

member, and know she was right."

"And you have remembered?"

"I didn't have to. I knew – that day – that it was my love that was fighting you, defending myself, wanting you to appreciate me, longing for you to love me. You never let me guess that you cared about me in that way at all."

"I tried to tell you when I kissed you."

"And I thought I must have told *you*. But afterwards you called it an experiment."

"One has to begin somewhere!"

"And you let it end there. Almost at once you were tempting Saskia away from Dirk. What was I to think?"

Axel bit his lip, pretending to look abashed. "I'm rather afraid – just what I intended you to think. I told you there were side-issues to my cultivation of Saskia, didn't I? Well, as Grethe pointed out, a little jealousy is a good bait with which to net a girl, and as I knew you were already jealous of Saskia over things she flaunted at you – skating, clothes, glamour, men – I agreed that jealousy of her over me wouldn't do you any harm."

"You needn't have troubled. I was already firmly hooked. But Tante Grethe seems to have been deep in all this with you, when I thought she was wasting her time, matchmaking for me all on her own."

"Deep? She has been in it right up to her chubby neck," Axel declared. "But you must forgive her. She has always meant that you and Dirk should marry Hollanders, and even with Munt, she usually gets her way. Besides, you haven't been entirely innocent yourself of guile – flaunting Mervyn Hawke at me, and pretending to Grethe that you weren't interested."

"Mervyn wasn't important in that way, and did you expect me to admit to Tante Grethe that I was in love with you?"

"It would have solved a lot if you had. But I'm glad you saved it to admit to me, my honey-coloured girl. Because that is what you are saying, isn't it? That you love me, *love* me, love *me*? As I love you – and more? Come here. Stand up. Let me kiss you properly –"

He kissed her properly – if that meant with abandon, with passion, all of himself that he had to offer her, speaking in the pressure of his lips and his clasp of her body – a fierce, possessive claiming of her which at last quietened to gentleness in his smoothing of her hair and the touch of his fingers tracing the contours of her brow, her cheeks, her jaw and the line of her throat.

A long time passed, filled, as far as talk went, with the little half-murmurs and incoherencies of lovers, their need of words far less urgent than their need to enjoy and to promise with look and touch and the sweet silence of embrace.

At last they stood apart, pleased with themselves, utterly happy. Swinging hands with her, Axel said, "That was better than fighting, wasn't it?"

"Much," she agreed. "Do you suppose we shan't fight any more from now on?"

He grinned. "Leopards and spots. Of course we shall fight – and enjoy it. Anyway, worship you as I may from ground level, I'm not building you a pedestal. Pedestals gather dust."

Jonnet laughed. "The very last thing our relationship is likely to gather, I'd say. But 'leopards and spots' to you! Do you really expect me to believe, with your record, that you are never going to look with calculating interest at any other girl?"

He frowned, considering that. "A first look, perhaps. Even a first thought. But no. No seconds, while I have you to have and to hold – Not to mention Frederic and Klaus and Truda and Jan–"

"Not to mention *who*?"

"*Whom*, dear, *whom*. Are you so Dutch already that you are forgetting your English grammar? F. and K. and T. and J. – our children, of course. I shall have them to have and to hold too."

"Not all at once, I hope!"

"No, but all in good time. And all of them blonde and grey-eyed–"

"Blue –"

"All right. Two of each," he conceded, and after a peck of a kiss for the tip of her nose, "And now, if it isn't too earthy of me to mention it, I'm hungry. What about you?"

"I hadn't realised it. But yes, I am."

"Then let's go and see what Grethe can offer us for supper, shall we?"

Jonnet warned, laughing, "I know what there was to be for supper and it wasn't caviare and roast swan."

"Well, to be strictly truthful, nor was it on the Herengracht, but in our state of euphoria, cold rabbit stew should be ambrosia enough." He put an arm round her. "And so – on our way to break the news to Grethe."

"And to Munt –"

"And naturally, also to Munt."

"Who accused me, the very first time we met, of wanting to oust Tante Grethe and him from the farm, and of having come to Holland in order to 'hang out my broom'," Jonnet giggled.

At that Axel threw back his head and shouted with laughter. "Well, now you can show him to what purpose you hung out your broom, and tell him that you have chosen to take up residence in quite another home – mine."

Looking down at her with the old mischief in his eyes — "Are you going to save me from having to rattle in it any longer, my woman?" he asked.

It was a question they had both answered already.

Each month from Harlequin

8 NEW FULL LENGTH ROMANCE NOVELS

Listed below are the last three months' releases:

1873	A PAVEMENT OF PEARL, Iris Danbury
1874	DESIGN FOR DESTINY, Sue Peters
1875	A PLUME OF DUST, Wynne May
1876	GATE OF THE GOLDEN GAZELLE, Dorothy Cork
1877	MEANS TO AN END, Lucy Gillen
1878	ISLE OF DREAMS, Elizabeth Dawson
1879	DARK VIKING, Mary Wibberley
1880	SWEET SUNDOWN, Margaret Way
1881	THE END OF THE RAINBOW, Betty Neels
1882	RIDE OUT THE STORM, Jane Donnelley
1883	AUTUMN CONCERTO, Rebecca Stratton
1884	THE GOLD OF NOON, Essie Summers
1885	PROUD CITADEL, Elizabeth Hoy
1886	TAKE ALL MY LOVES, Janice Gray
1887	LOVE AND LUCY BROWN, Joyce Dingwell
1888	THE BONDS OF MATRIMONY, Elizabeth Hunter
1889	REEDS OF HONEY, Margaret Way
1890	TELL ME MY FORTUNE, Mary Burchell
1891	SCORCHED WINGS, Elizabeth Ashton
1892	THE HOUSE CALLED SAKURA, Katrina Britt
1893	IF DREAMS CAME TRUE, Rozella Lake
1894	QUICKSILVER SUMMER, Dorothy Cork
1895	GLEN OF SIGHS, Lucy Gillen
1896	THE WIDE FIELDS OF HOME, Jane Arbor

These titles are available at your local bookseller, or through the Harlequin Reader Service, M.P.O. Box 707, Niagara Falls, N.Y. 14302; Canadian address 649 Ontario St., Stratford, Ont.

L

Have You Missed Any of These *Harlequin Romances?*

- ☐ 771 NURSE PRUE IN CEYLON
  Gladys Fullbrook
- ☐ 772 CHLOE WILDE, STUDENT
  NURSE, Joan Turner
- ☐ 787 THE TWO FACES OF NURSE
  ROBERTS, Nora Sanderson
- ☐ 790 SOUTH TO THE SUN
  Betty Beaty
- ☐ 794 SURGEON'S RETURN
  Hilda Nickson
- ☐ 812 FACTORY NURSE   Hilary Neal
- ☐ 825 MAKE UP YOUR MIND NURSE
  Phyllis Matthewman
- ☐ 841 TRUANT HEART
  Patricia Fenwick
  (Original Harlequin title
  "Doctor In Brazil")
- ☐ 858 MY SURGEON NEIGHBOUR
  Jane Arbor
- ☐ 873 NURSE JULIE OF WARD
  THREE   Joan Callender
- ☐ 878 THIS KIND OF LOVE
  Kathryn Blair
- ☐ 890 TWO SISTERS
  Valerie K. Nelson

- ☐ 897 NURSE HILARY'S HOLIDAY
  TASK, Jan Haye
- ☐ 900 THERE CAME A SURGEON
  Hilda Pressley
- ☐ 901 HOPE FOR TOMORROW
  Anne Weale
- ☐ 902 MOUNTAIN OF DREAMS
  Barbara Rowan
- ☐ 903 SO LOVED AND SO FAR
  Elizabeth Hoy
- ☐ 907 HOMECOMING HEART
  Joan Blair
  (Original Harlequin title
  "Two for the Doctor")
- ☐ 909 DESERT DOORWAY
  Pamela Kent
- ☐ 911 RETURN OF SIMON
  Celine Conway
- ☐ 912 THE DREAM AND THE
  DANCER, Eleanor Farnes
- ☐ 919 DEAR INTRUDER
  Jane Arbor
- ☐ 936 TIGER HALL
  Esther Wyndham

PLEASE NOTE: All Harlequin Romances from #1857 onwards are 75c. Books below that number, **where available** are priced at 60c through Harlequin Reader Service until December 31st, 1975.

**TO: HARLEQUIN READER SERVICE, Dept. N 507
M.P.O. Box 707, Niagara Falls, N.Y. 14302
Canadian address: Stratford, Ont., Canada**

- ☐ Please send me the free Harlequin Romance Catalogue.
- ☐ Please send me the titles checked.

I enclose $_____ (No C.O.D.'s). All books listed are 60c each. To help defray postage and handling cost, please add 25c.

Name _____

Address _____

City/Town _____

State/Prov. _____ Zip _____

AA-2

Have You Missed Any of These
Harlequin Romances?

- [ ] 941 MAYENGA FARM
  Kathryn Blair
- [ ] 945 DOCTOR SANDY
  Margaret Malcolm
- [ ] 948 ISLANDS OF SUMMER
  Anne Weale
- [ ] 951 THE ENCHANTED TRAP
  Kate Starr
- [ ] 957 NO LEGACY FOR LINDSAY
  Essie Summers
- [ ] 965 CAME A STRANGER
  Celine Conway
- [ ] 968 SWEET BRENDA
  Penelope Walsh
- [ ] 974 NIGHT OF THE HURRICANE
  Andrea Blake
- [ ] 984 ISLAND IN THE DAWN
  Averil Ives
- [ ] 993 SEND FOR NURSE ALISON
  Marjorie Norrell
- [ ] 994 JUBILEE HOSPITAL
  Jan Tempest
- [ ] 1001 NO PLACE FOR SURGEONS
  Elizabeth Gilzean
- [ ] 1004 THE PATH OF THE
  MOONFISH, Betty Beaty
- [ ] 1009 NURSE AT FAIRCHILDS
  Marjorie Norrell
- [ ] 1010 DOCTOR OF RESEARCH
  Elizabeth Houghton
- [ ] 1011 THE TURQUOISE SEA
  Hilary Wilde
- [ ] 1018 HOSPITAL IN THE TROPICS
  Gladys Fullbrook
- [ ] 1019 FLOWER OF THE MORNING
  Celine Conway
- [ ] 1024 THE HOUSE OF DISCONTENT
  Esther Wyndham
- [ ] 1048 HIGH MASTER OF CLERE
  Jane Arbor
- [ ] 1052 MEANT FOR EACH OTHER
  Mary Burchell
- [ ] 1074 NEW SURGEON AT ST.
  LUCIAN'S, Elizabeth
  Houghton
- [ ] 1087 A HOME FOR JOCELYN
  Eleanor Farnes
- [ ] 1094 MY DARK RAPPAREE
  Henrietta Reid

- [ ] 1098 THE UNCHARTED OCEAN
  Margaret Malcolm
- [ ] 1102 A QUALITY OF MAGIC
  Rose Burghley
- [ ] 1106 WELCOME TO PARADISE
  Jill Tahourdin
- [ ] 1115 THE ROMANTIC HEART
  Norrey Ford
- [ ] 1120 HEART IN HAND
  Margaret Malcolm
- [ ] 1121 TEAM DOCTOR, Ann Gilmour
- [ ] 1122 WHISTLE AND I'LL COME
  Flora Kidd
- [ ] 1138 LOVING IS GIVING
  Mary Burchell
- [ ] 1144 THE TRUANT BRIDE
  Sara Seale
- [ ] 1150 THE BRIDE OF MINGALAY
  Jean S. Macleod
- [ ] 1166 DOLAN OF SUGAR HILLS
  Kate Starr
- [ ] 1172 LET LOVE ABIDE
  Norrey Ford
- [ ] 1182 GOLDEN APPLE ISLAND
  Jane Arbor
- [ ] 1183 NEVER CALL IT LOVING
  Marjorie Lewty
- [ ] 1184 THE HOUSE OF OLIVER
  Jean S. Macleod
- [ ] 1200 SATIN FOR THE BRIDE
  Kate Starr
- [ ] 1201 THE ROMANTIC DR. RYDON
  Anne Durham
- [ ] 1209 THE STUBBORN DR STEPHEN
  Elizabeth Houghton
- [ ] 1211 BRIDE OF KYLSAIG
  Iris Danbury
- [ ] 1214 THE MARSHALL FAMILY
  Mary Burchell
- [ ] 1216 ORANGES AND LEMONS
  Isobel Chace
- [ ] 1218 BEGGARS MAY SING
  Sara Seale
- [ ] 1222 DARK CONFESSOR
  Elinor Davis
- [ ] 1236 JEMIMA
  Leonora Starr

BB

Have You Missed Any of These
Harlequin Romances?

- ☐ 1246 THE CONSTANT HEART
  Eleanor Farnes
- ☐ 1248 WHERE LOVE IS
  Norrey Ford
- ☐ 1253 DREAM COME TRUE
  Patricia Fenwick
- ☐ 1276 STEEPLE RIDGE
  Jill Tahourdin
- ☐ 1277 STRANGER'S TRESPASS
  Jane Arbor
- ☐ 1282 THE SHINING STAR
  Hilary Wilde
- ☐ 1284 ONLY MY HEART TO GIVE
  Nan Asquith
- ☐ 1288 THE LAST OF THE KINTYRES
  Catherine Airlie
- ☐ 1293 I KNOW MY LOVE
  Sara Seale
- ☐ 1309 THE HILLS OF MAKETU
  Gloria Bevan
- ☐ 1312 PEPPERCORN HARVEST
  Ivy Ferrari
- ☐ 1601 THE NEWCOMER
  Hilda Pressley
- ☐ 1607 NOT LESS THAN ALL
  Margaret Malcolm
- ☐ 1718 LORD OF THE FOREST
  Hilda Nickson
- ☐ 1722 FOLLOW A STRANGER
  Charlotte Lamb
- ☐ 1725 THE EXTRAORDINARY EN-
  GAGEMENT Marjorie Lewty
- ☐ 1726 MAN IN CHARGE, Lilian Feake
- ☐ 1729 THE YOUNG DOCTOR
  Sheila Douglas
- ☐ 1730 FLAME IN FIJI, Gloria Bevan
- ☐ 1731 THE FORBIDDEN VALLEY
  Essie Summers
- ☐ 1732 BEYOND THE SUNSET
  Flora Kidd
- ☐ 1733 CALL AND I'LL COME
  Mary Burchell
- ☐ 1734 THE GIRL FROM ROME
  Nan Asquith
- ☐ 1735 TEMPTATIONS OF THE MOON
  Hilary Wilde
- ☐ 1736 THE ENCHANTED RING
  Lucy Gillen

- ☐ 1737 WINTER OF CHANGE
  Betty Neels
- ☐ 1738 THE MUTUAL LOOK
  Joyce Dingwell
- ☐ 1739 BELOVED ENEMY
  Mary Wibberley
- ☐ 1740 ROMAN SUMMER
  Jane Arbor
- ☐ 1741 MOORLAND MAGIC
  Elizabeth Ashton
- ☐ 1743 DESTINY IS A FLOWER
  Stella Frances Nel
- ☐ 1744 WINTER LOVING
  Janice Gray
- ☐ 1745 NURSE AT NOONGWALLA
  Roumelia Lane
- ☐ 1746 WITHOUT ANY AMAZEMENT
  Margaret Malcolm
- ☐ 1748 THE GOLDEN MADONNA
  Rebecca Stratton
- ☐ 1749 LOVELY IS THE ROSE
  Belinda Dell
- ☐ 1750 THE HOUSE OF THE SCISSORS
  Isobel Chace
- ☐ 1751 CARNIVAL COAST
  Charlotte Lamb
- ☐ 1752 MIRANDA'S MARRIAGE
  Margery Hilton
- ☐ 1753 TIME MAY CHANGE
  Nan Asquith
- ☐ 1754 THE PRETTY WITCH
  Lucy Gillen
- ☐ 1755 SCHOOL MY HEART
  Penelope Walsh
- ☐ 1756 AN APPLE IN EDEN
  Kay Thorpe
- ☐ 1757 THE GIRL AT SALTBUSH FLAT
  Dorothy Cork
- ☐ 1758 THE CRESCENT MOON
  Elizabeth Hunter
- ☐ 1759 THE REST IS MAGIC
  Marjorie Lewty
- ☐ 1760 THE GUARDED GATES
  Katrina Britt
- ☐ 1780 THE TOWER OF THE WINDS
  Elizabeth Hunter
- ☐ 1783 CINDERELLA IN MINK
  Roberta Leigh

CC